To my Eleven Friends,

Thank you for your continued strength and support

Michael Andrew McDonald

OTHER ACCOUNTS BY THE AUTHOR

Immortalim: The Journey

Immortalim: The War

From the Books of CURRENTEERS:

The Star Current

Pirates of Salari

Echo Plague

Dreathlocked

Supernova Flare

Eternities' Reach

Shadow's Light

Quicksaber

Immortalim

The CALL

Michael Andrew McDonald

Michael Andrew McDonald
Acknowledgements:

Eteuyati Salanoa, Mark Bott, Taylor Moore, Parker Standing, Jordan Mullins, Benjamin Epperson, Jaden Johnson, Courtlan Wilcox, Nicholas Squires, Christopher Willis, Bradley Snow, and Dallin Zollinger—some for directly assisting the writing, all for helping me to find more of who I am;
Special thanks to James and Vicki Matsumori, also Peter and Heather Cooke;
Foster Bateman, the Faithful Beta Reader;
Especial thanks to D.J. Stevenson for his cover art;
And countless others who have contributed helpful tips and support, directly and indirectly!

With special thanks to Brian Jacques, C.S. Lewis, and Richard Bach, who inspired this work.

Immortalim: The Call

Printing history:
Original softcover edition / 2017
Electronic edition / 2017

Visit the Currenteers' Facebook at
https://www.facebook.com/TheStarCurrent/

ISBN: 9781549533075

All interior artwork is the author's own

To the One I call Master,

My only lasting mentor

Michael Andrew McDonald

Foreword

It has been so long ago that these events surrounding my origins have occurred; but the story isn't just my own, but also that of my eleven other friends. All of us comprise what's known as the Immortalims. Well, technically Preservants, but you'll soon be able to sort that out!

Ah, history records things a little differently than they really happened; some events are exaggerated, while others are omitted entirely. Given the hero worship that so prevalently laces the stories on the worlds we care for, I have opted to set aside some time to tell things as they really happened. Regardless of how fantastic it all seems, it is true. We actually are over five Millennia old; some of us have lived a life of low diversity, appearing as one of a pawful of species; others have been well over a score of different creatures throughout Time. Some of us only visit two of the Seven Worlds, perhaps three; others have been to them all. Given that I am the Traveler, I hold the record for the greatest quantity of species and visits by far! Then again, when it comes to bragging rights about anything done over the centuries, I cannot claim the record for the number of lives saved as the Warrior can, nor the number of grey hairs inflicted by the Rogue. Unfortunately, he does pride himself in that...

My underlying purpose in telling these stories (setting aside the clarification of a few details) is to show that our world is filled with so much more wonder than we can appreciate; there are forces at work under the supreme guidance of the Creator that have aided us in these last five millennia. It is not just our lives that have been accompanied by these occurrences, justfully dubbed as miracles; we see it in the lives of everyone that we meet. Unlike the shorter-lived acquaintances of ours, we happen to have become very keen at recognizing them. As I write my tale, I invite you to watch for these subtle clues, both within my account, and in your own lives. Miracles, by definition, defy all common sense; and interestingly, so do most of the laws of nature, discovered by the genius minds of Earth over the last five centuries. I say then that miracles are everywhere! Just watch for them.

Now, I get on with my record: Watch for the messages contained herein. There is no sense in ignoring advice from an undying, shape-shifting old chap that has

Michael Andrew McDonald

traversed seven worlds and the many cultures they've

spawned, is there?

-8-

-9-

Michael Andrew McDonald

Prologue

Ela and his twin sister Roath scrambled over one another to be the first to see their newborn brother. The young syan lad was in the lead once their father had given the word that they now had a younger sibling; however, Ela had stumbled as a stray tree root protruding from the floor caught his paw, sending him sprawling with a yelp.

"Oof!"

His sister dashed past with a smug look, though a stern glance from their father stopped Roath in her tracks.

"Please," he gently hissed, motioning with a nod towards the blanket where his mate lay. "He's sleeping. You don't want to waken your brother, either of you."

He waited for an indication that they understood him. Their heads bobbed obediently as Ela picked himself up, though quietly. They three made their way over to the mother's side, where she was curled up on a soft blanket interwoven with triangular symbols.

Resting against the belly of his protective mother, the newborn syannett slept soundly. He had stirred slightly from the noise of his elder siblings' entrance, but had resumed a peaceful slumber. His mother nuzzled him lightly with her nose, and glanced up at her mate.

"What will be a good name for him, Kahren?"

He nodded thoughtfully, stroking his whiskers as he usually did when pondering. "I think he must be named Alamanthea... *Beloved Brother.*"

"Really? Will that be his name?" Roath asked excitedly. She was again silenced by a stern glance.

"Keep your voice down, lass," the noble male syan replied in a low tone, careful himself not to wake the slumbering infant. He turned again to his mate. "Will that name fit?"

She smiled again and lovingly nuzzled her kit, scooping him up in her arms as she sat upright, disturbing his sleep outrightly. He mewled himself awake in mild protest, his squeaks drawing the full attention of his elder siblings. They gazed upon him in wide-eyed wonder as their mother confirmed the name in order to complete the simple ceremony.

"Aye, then. My son Alamanthea, welcome to the world."

It was on that day that Ela felt the sparks of brotherly love deepen as he watched his sibling's eyes open for the first time.

Chapter 1

"Come on Alam, hurry up! Don't be all day about it!"

Many seasons later, on a pleasantly warm late-summer morning, Kahren led his two eldest sons Ela and Alamanthea up the slope of a mountain not too far from their home. On the foothills of the great lone megalith, they followed a northbound path whose course led through the trees, walking since an hour past dawn. By this time, Kahren had many more sons, although only these two were grown and responsible enough to navigate the treacherous trail they now walked. Ela had already gone this way before on many an occasion, but his brother as of yet had not. This was his first time, hence his elder brother pestering him roguishly.

Alam slid back several paces, the loose gravel shuffling under his paws. He glowered ahead to his brother's grinning.

"No fair, Ela!" Alamanthea shot back. "Perhaps if you'd point out the area to step, it would go a lot more quickly."

Kahren turned, his ears and whiskers twitching with amusement. He stood a score of paces ahead of his sons as he called back, a hefty walking staff helping him keep his balance as he probed for the safest parts of the trail to go up. He adjusted his shoulder pack as he chided with humor.

"Alamanth, he *is* telling you. You just haven't been paying attention."

Ela nodded to his younger brother with another playful grin. The young syan shook his head in confusion. "What do you mean, 'He's been telling me?' The only words I've heard coming from his smelly trap is to hurry it up!"

Kahren chuckled to himself. "None of that, now. Just follow Ela's pawsteps. He's only stepping where it's safe, relatively the same course we've always taken. Not everything needs to be said in words to get a message across."

Alamanth quickly fell in line behind his elder brother, his face beet-red with embarrassment for not having figured that out sooner. A heavy silence fell as they continued onward. Ahead, the gravel portion of the trail went for over a hundred paces more before it would become a smooth dusty path.

The rest of the afternoon continued on uneventfully. By the time the sun began to sink low on the horizon, they were in a clearing nearly a third of the way up the mountain's side, where the incline rose more sharply, at about the elevation where the rocky mass fed into jagged points.

Ela's younger brother was exhausted. He flopped himself upon a nearby rock jutting up out of the ground along off to the side of the clearing. He rested upon his paws, his sides heaving and gasping. Meanwhile, the older male syan had silently begun assembling a quick campsite with the aid of his other son. Within moments, a circle was cleared of pine-needles, fallen leaves, and other forest debris that littered the wooded hollow. Some of the sticks and twigs were soon being consumed in the crackle of a pinewood fire, smoke rising up through the sparse leafy boughs above. Twilight was well underway.

Alam finally slowed his breathing to even out. He straightened up, his form still slightly hunched. As he took a step to turn towards the makeshift firepit, he winced. Ela, sitting upon a fallen log facing the flames glanced toward his brother, grinning and shaking his head.

"What, a simple hike like that got the best of you, has it? You seem pretty beaten."

Kahren raised an eyebrow at the comment, poking the flames with a well-used fire hardened stick. "Now, now, son; you didn't take the trail so well *your* first try either."

Ela glanced up to meet his father's serious gaze, his focus primarily upon the crackle and warmth before him. He briefly rubbed his paws together and held them forward. "Well, that makes the three of us, then."

Kahren gave his eldest a quizzical look. "What do you mean?"

"Mother told me how exhausted you were when you first returned from this trail. It sounded bad from the description I heard."

Kahren glanced up to the stars, silent for a long, awkward moment. He then stared back at his sons, meeting the two sets of eyes watching him. Alam was at his brother's side when their father spoke almost solemnly.

"My sons, there is a reason for that. Sure, the strain of the journey was great. Aye, the trail was no different then than it is now. But, what happened at the top of that peak to our north was something profound, something personal, and something most of all, draining."

He nodded in the general direction of the looming mountain top backlit by a canopy of stars. His sons leaned in close, ears perked intently. Kahren shook his head.

"No. Perhaps another night I will tell you what happened."

However, the disappointed fallen looks on their faces instantly changed the Patriarch syan's mind. He shook his head again, this time smiling in fatherly kindness.

"Perhaps you two have waited long enough. But do

remember, what I'm about to share with you is sacred. It is never to be taken lightly or with jesting. And do not mention it with your other siblings until I have told them. Are you both ready to take on that kind of responsibility?"

He glanced between his sons, his face dead serious. He waited until their heads bobbed up and down obediently.

"Okay, then," Kahren began. "I will share some of the things I saw and heard, but I won't tell either of you everything, you'll see it for yourself soon enough."

The older syan sighed thoughtfully as he continued. In the background, crickets chirruped rapidly. "It was many seasons ago when I first decided to venture away from the holt. This was not long afore Ela and Roath were born. Your mother was never really the restless roaming kind, so I would usually go at it alone. Eventually my wanderings brought me here, to this mountain." He motioned again, his paw sweeping the surrounding trees. After a brief pause to allow this all to sink in, he continued.

"After a few days, I managed to make my way to the summit's top. When I got there, I was very terribly exhausted, for I had taken the long hard way up another side."

"Then why did you bother going up if it was so hard, Father?" Alam interrupted. Kahren sent a glance up to the none-too-distant peak as he leaned back slightly on the log.

"I may never know exactly why, to be honest. Something was drawing me to it. Something on that mountain was calling to me in my dreams. And so I went.

"Now, back to where I was: It was late in the evening by the time I laid on the mountain's height. I was so drained that I could not remain very conscious after seeing the most breathtaking sunset I have ever witnessed in all my life. Shortly thereafter, I fell into a very deep sleep.

"What finally woke me was soreness coursing through my body. Though I really didn't want to get up, that calling feeling that had been pulling me here had returned, and was stronger than ever, now telling me to arise."

Kahren paused, glancing up longingly towards the stars beyond the peak. Though normally stern, the two syan lads—the elder a near-adult—could tell that their father was beginning to become emotional, a rare occurrence. The reason became evident as the older syan continued.

"The instant I shakily stood upon my footpaws, some unearthly power came upon me. Though it was well into the depths of night, I suddenly was surrounded by a river of light, so bright and brilliant that the sun would be put to shame. As I'm sure you both can imagine, my sons, I was taken by surprise and nearly collapsed again. However, I found that I was then filled with a new, awesome strength, the likes of which I have never before felt, nor ever since.

"While trying to make sense of it all, I soon became aware that I was not alone in that river of brightness. Another creature had appeared and stood right before me, enveloped by a myriad of colors and brilliant light, similar but greater in luster than what then surrounded me. Despite my attempts to identify the creature spirit, I could simply not see what species they were, so intense was the appearance, like lightning. That was when he spoke."

"What did he say, father?" asked Ela intently. Both

brothers awaited a response, as Kahren was once again silent for a long moment. The flames of the firepit before them had grown lower, but they took little heed. The patriarch swallowed hard before continuing.

"He called my name, first of all. That is what he did, oh aye, sure as I'm speaking to you, he sounded as though he knew me. He then told me that he had been sent from the Creator, and that he had a message for me. He said...ahem, sorry... that I had a rare task and privilege to perform. The spirit then gave me this prophecy, which I cannot forget; it is forever seared into my memory:

"'Twain leaders shall arise,

These search thy fam'ly line:

The first in wandering, the second doth prize,

Their lives thou must refine.'

"He then continued to give me further knowledge, but that I cannot share with you now, or at all tonight. It will be given to both of you soon enough. Words cannot describe, nor do it any justice, anyway. When the bright creature finished giving me his message, he left, disappearing before my very eyes. The only thing that remained was the strength that I was given."

"Really? It was still there?" asked Alam in surprise. "It didn't just vanish?"

Kahren nodded. "Correct. I waited for a few hours more, but decided that I was not going to receive another such visit, and so tried to return a shorter way to the holt. I soon found that my lingering was unwise on my part.

"As I made my way down the mountain's side, the great strength began to wane away. Regardless of how far I went, or how often I stopped, I began to become weaker, and by the time that I returned home, I was barely conscious of anything. So Ela, I didn't just get exhausted the first time I ventured up this mountain; I was drained. Since then, I discovered this particular path, which makes it all the easier to trek to the mountain peak."

Ela and Alamanth exchanged glances, unsure at first what to think of their father's story. Kahren once again stared up at the stars longingly. Whether he was aware of their puzzled looks, they could not tell. However, as he had mentioned, there was clearly more that he was not telling that Ela now desperately wanted to know.

But alas, he dared not express the desire, knowing how stern his father could be once he had already made up his mind; he already stated that they were to wait and see. The young adult syan came to the self-realization that if his father was right about how marvelous the experience was, being beyond words, it would be better to wait anyway.

Ela reached down toward the stack of wood to put more branches on the fire, but this brought his father back to reality, who motioned with his paw to let the flames die down.

"No, son. Let the last few bits be consumed. It is about time to rest ourselves for the night anyway. We have a long day ahead of us tomorrow."

Within moments, the three syans had sleeping blankets rolled out near the fire pit, adjacently opposite the logs. As Alamanth laid his head down, he glanced to Kahren, whose dimly lit form stretched himself into a resting position.

"Father?" he asked.

"Aye, son?"

There was a brief pause before Alam continued. "Will you and mother always be around?"

Kahren had laid with his back to him. He sighed heavily as a passing breeze rustled his mane.

"Why do you ask?"

Alam paused again. "Well, a few nights ago, I had a dream that there was something horrible happening. Many creatures that I saw were fighting viciously. There was a most awful feeling in the air. All three of us were there, but I didn't see others of our family. I saw that something had happened to Ela during it all, and you had taken him to safety, just before you were attacked by a shadowy figure. It was terrible."

Ela shook his head from his own resting position. "It does sound bad, but you should stop worrying about it, Alam. Like you said, it was just a dream. It couldn't possibly really happen." He scoffed lightheartedly. "Right, father? Father?"

Both lads glanced toward the older syan, whose side was rising and falling evenly with his slowed breathing. While it seemed he was asleep, there was a lack of snoring that told them otherwise. Realizing that their father obviously didn't want to discuss the dream, possibly because they would be getting up early the next morning, Ela and Alam shut their eyes and waited for sleep to overtake them.

Chapter 2

Dawn the next morning came like a glowing sentinel peering over the horizon. Golden rays of sunlight bathed the mountaintop, sweeping across the landscape, the darkness of night fleeing for all it was worth. Nocturnal creatures had long since gone to their rest, while all other creatures were beginning to arise to greet the coming day. Flocks of geese had already begun to migrate south at the early prospect of winter. On occasion, as the chevron formations glided across the sky, noble-looking creatures called okara would flap their wings, their weasellike forms rising to meet the geese, flying alongside them. However, this would result in the formation falling into chaos, accompanied by angry and irritated honking. The okara, unfazed by the aggressive behavior, would coolly fly away, either to land and begin grazing in the grassy fields below, or returning out of boredom to pester other migrating groups.

It was this honking that awoke Ela from sleep. Since the conversation the previous night, he too had been plagued with the same dreams his brother had had. As the distant noise of irritated fowl died down, he struggled to recall the vivid images.

Ela found himself alongside his father, with Alam a stone's throw away. The trio was in the midst of a terrible fight taking place in a dark vine enshrouded stone amphitheater. He saw his younger brother deftly avoiding blows from a small pale-furred creature donning a torn blue garment. The attacker's stubby but quick black paws flew rapidly in combat, but Alam miraculously anticipated every move. With a start, Ela knew that the attacker was a male gara, despite never having seen one before.

Kahren bounded and leapt to the rescue. With a tremendous heave, the syan's paws locked squarely upward on the gara's scrawny form. With a yell of surprise, the gara flew, hitting the stony wall with a sickening thud. The unfortunate creature fell to the ground, clearly slain from the blow.

Meanwhile, Ela had watched the whole event, completely and momentarily distracted from the fighting happening all around him. Without warning, a large grey-furred beast with a long whippy tail was tossed through the air by a wolverine, striking the young syan hard in the back.

Both rolled down the gentle incline on the ground towards an overhang of ivy. As Ela came to a stop, he tried to rise up on his paws, but a sharp twinge of pain shot through his body. He collapsed, completely helpless.

Almost immediately, his father was by his side, and began dragging Ela to safety in the ivy. The young syan gasped in pain, but as he glanced towards the unconscious form of the body that had hit him, he recognized the creature's face, and knew that he was a young hollow about his own age. Again, he had never met one. Had it not been for the seriousness of the situation, he would have wondered why his father had never shown him some of these species, considering how often the two had traveled to other lands.

Once Ela was hidden in the leafy ground foliage, his father gave him a saddened look and darted away into the melee.

It was then that Ela had awakened from sleep. Though some details of the dream he could not distinctly recall, it still disturbed him, especially since he knew things he shouldn't, such as about the gara and the hollow. He'd heard of them, even though he had never seen any. Despite the fact that it was definitely a dream, it all seemed so real.

Still anxiously trying to shake off the effects of sleep, the young male syan glanced around at his surroundings. He slowly realized that his father's resting blanket was empty. Ela turned and shook his sleeping brother awake.

"Alam, wake up!" he gently hissed. The young syan blinked into confused wakefulness.

"What is it?" he asked. Looking around, he too saw that their father was gone. Both lads slowly stood up scanning the clearing. However, it was in vain. Kahren was nowhere to be seen, and there was no indication of where he had gone.

"Where is he?" Alam asked in a whisper.

"I dunno. I barely just woke up myself," he replied. "Let's try to look for him. You go east, and I'll head west." He nodded his head each direction and began to go.

"Wait, shouldn't we go together?" asked Alam. Ela momentarily turned to face him.

"We'll cover twice as much area this way. Oh, and be sure not to go too far. And stay within sight of the clearing, if possible."

"What should I do if I find father?"

"Just call for me. Since we have limited time to get up to the top before nightfall, if you don't see him by midmorning, when the sun is about there in the sky," Ela held up his paw diagonally, "Then return here, since he'll likely have come back by then. Try not to call out for father, he may just be meditating. Anything else? Right then, let's go!"

True to Ela's anticipation, Kahren was away from the camp for early morning meditation. He sat cross-legged upon a rock slab perched over a steep slope of the mountain, which allowed for a breathtaking view of their holt in the encompassing forest of the valley below.

The remark from his son the night before troubled him deeply. Not only had Alam usually shown remarkable ability of foresight in the past, but the description sounded so familiar, that it plagued Kahren's mind. The aged male syan hated it when he was so disturbed. It had caused a nearly sleepless night, leaving him to wonder where he had heard something like those events before. Just over an hour before dawn, he had decided to get away from the snoring of his sons to think, sleep having long since fled from his eyes.

As dawn had come and gone, Kahren was so absorbed in his ponderings that he was not aware of the approaching pawsteps of Alam. Before his son was even at his side, he was experiencing vivid flashbacks of his own dreams.

He was holding Ela's limp form close in front of him. The syans were in the gnarly roots of the holt, Kahren trying hard not to make contact with the horrified stare of his mate as she stood before him. He gently set his son on the earthen floor, still supporting the almost lifeless form. Ela's eyelids were shut tight, and he was having difficulty breathing. What really drew Kahren's attention was that his son's side was tightly bandaged with a makeshift dressing that was covered and soaked with blood.

His mate's motherly instinct kicking in, she

immediately came to her firstborn son's side where he lay.

"Kahren, what happened?" She cried in heart-wrenching anguish.

Then the dreams skipped on. *Kahren saw only war, death, and destruction surrounding him. In a wide spacious field, there were thousands of creatures of numerous kinds locked in mortal combat, few being spared of death. Many fought tooth and claw, some bearing weapons. The nearby ring of mountains loomed ominously high in the dark and hazy sky.*

He looked on and saw Ela in the heat of battle, fighting with a maddened energy which Kahren had never witnessed in any creature before. There was something different about his eldest son. He was fighting with a staff, moving so quickly that he should have long ago fallen with exhaustion, but nonetheless he kept going. It was an almost frightening contrast to the half-dead state that Kahren had witnessed earlier.

Rain had begun to fall upon the strewn carcasses lying about, many creatures falling to the angry blows of their foes. Lightning flashed through the sky overhead, the glowing forks of electricity fading as thunder rent the air, so loudly that it was a miracle that the very rocks did not shatter to pieces.

Yet, despite the storm, the fighting did not cease, nor did the combatants even seem to notice. Instead, they continued fighting with what seemed to be even more ferocity. The small puddles of rain water that pooled ran red with the blood of many creatures: stoats, weasels, rats, the compact bodied Gara, otters, hares, squirrels, the occasional odd species, and oftimes a syan or two. Their screams of battle were nearly drowned out by the pounding thunder, their cries of injury and pain soon silenced by fatal blows and stabs of death.

In the midst of it all, Kahren was confused as to why this work of destruction all around him was happening. He had never before seen such anger and violence in his life. What would cause such a thing, *he wondered silently to himself.*

His thoughts were broken as his son Alam stood before him. Being disoriented by the dream-turned-vision, Kahren at first lost track of where he was. A moment of hurried glancing about soon refocused his mind back to reality.

"Father?" asked Alam, "Are you all right? You look

very fearful."

His father quickly got up. "Never mind that. Where is your brother? Why aren't you two together?"

Alam pointed his paw towards the camp. "Ela went west to look for you when we arose this morning and found you gone. He told me to go east this direction, and to return to camp by midmorning if I had not yet found you. It's almost that time now."

Kahren's brow furrowed in puzzlement, and he glanced towards the sun's position at two hours past dawn. "Midmorning? Has it really been that long already?"

After a brief moment of careful thought, and not wanting his son to ask any more questions that might lead to the horrible lingering memory of the dreams, Kahren shook his head, muttering. "I guess I just lost track of how long I intended to meditate. Come, Alamanth, let's go find that brother of yours."

At that very same moment, an older male hollow glanced proudly into the sky. Holding a paw up to shield his pale crystal-blue eyes from the glare of the sun, he watched a small speck cross the blue over the nearby mountain, vanishing out of sight for the briefest of moments. It reappeared, and then grew rapidly as it approached the hollow's perch on the edge of a rock cliff overlooking a shallow river below. His long narrow muzzle, scrunched from anticipation, relaxed.

Wearing a haldris, a special garment woven with strange symbols, the silky fabric was so patterned that no one save hollows could see them directly. Anyone of another species who tried to look straight at the hypnotic weaving had their vision clouded, leaving the hollow wearers unseen, apt to their species' name. This allowed them to go wherever they pleased, so long as they wore the cloak garments, which bore hoods, sleeves, and folds that covered everything from the waist down.

Moaren was his name. Aside from the long whippy tail and the haldris, the remaining features consisted of a strong slender frame not unlike an okara's, and dull gray fur streaked with patches of a white winter coat that was forming steadily as autumn progressed. Only earlier that morning, Moaren decided that it would be the day that his firstborn son, eldest of the next generation of his tribe, would learn to ride an okara; after all, the skill not only had potential uses in the future, but it was also a visually impressive thing for an up-and-coming chieftain to do. And at the moment, he was doing it *very* well, as though he'd been riding for seasons.

There was a gust and flurry of enormous wings as the enlarging speck in the sky grew to be that mounted okara. Riding upon the noble creature's back was a young hollow, who used a naturally but immensely long tail that wound several times around the slender waist of the Okara like a safety harness. He maneuvered the flight just over the pointed eartips of the older hollow, who turned and called out after the airborne pair excitedly.

"Yaaahhh, Salari, that's the way!"

Salari guided the Okara upward and around in a loop, coming back in for a landing. His father stepped aside, allowing the flying pair to touchdown, turning about gracefully in the process. The young lad leapt high in the air off the okara's back as the winged creature came to a sudden halt at the edge of the cliff where Moaren had just stood. Salari landed upon all fours, but quickly stood upright, grinning at his father. Moaren nodded back with a smile of approval. His long fangs, jutting from under his lips, glinted in the light of the near midmorning sun as he praised his son's skill.

"Nicely done! That was outstanding talent you displayed. Your mother and I will be so proud as you show all those graceful abilities on the Mid-autumn Festival. My goodness, how the Creator has gifted you, my lad."

Salari was quickly the recipient of a hefty clap on the back. He gazed with determination at the Okara upon which he had ridden.

"Wasn't only me, father." He shook his head and motioning with a nod. "You've got to give Jehleen here some credit. It was his set of wings that took me up to the deep blue."

Moaren nodded approvingly. "True. Give credit where credit is due, eh?" With that, he gave his son another hearty clap. "Come lad. Mayhap we should return home now. You must surely be sore after that serious flying."

Salari cocked his head in agreement. As the twain padded away, Jehleen the Okara hesitated. Being a creature of silent prophecy, he sensed a dread building in the air. Something terrible would be happening soon.

Michael Andrew McDonald

The noble creature quickly ducked after his two hollows, hoping they hadn't noticed.

Chapter 3

As Alam and his father returned to the camp, they found Ela sitting casually over the dead remains of the previous night's fire. He was poking at the ashes, stirring up some still glowing red embers, attempting to place dry pine needles atop them to reignite the flames. However, as the needles began to catch afire, they began to put off wispy smoke so quickly, that it caught Ela by surprise as he glanced up. He fell backwards, gasping and choking from the fumes. Squinting and blinking as his eyes began to water, he grinned sheepishly at his father and brother, all the while trying to clear his throat in embarrassment.

"Ahem, oh, er, hello Father, I was just—" He coughed. "Er, well, you see, trying to bring the fire back, uh...”

Ela suddenly found himself a loss for words. He had expected his father to become stern; however, Kahren was slightly distant, almost somewhat anxious.

“Never you mind the fire. Here, throw dirt on it, and roll up your blankets. You too, Alam. We've already taken too long as it is to resume our journey. We must arrive at the mountain peak afore sundown. Come!”

Ela's twin sister Roath stood beside their mother just outside the entrance to their holt. Both female syans had been standing there since before dawn, watching the distant but nonetheless majestic mountainside. The simple dwelling in which they lived lay in the roots of a sarcras tree, the species of which was composed of a thick trunk, a wide sweeping root system and gnarly limbs whose branches usually sported wonderful amounts of a most delicious fruit in midsummer. During springtime in full swing, tender young petals of diverse flowers shot forth along the sides of the path that snaked its way through the forest shortly after the last traces of winter had melted away for the first time. It had been a cold harsh ice season. Thankfully, the seven winters since had treated the country more kindly.

Having lost track of time, their silent vigil was interrupted by several of Roath's siblings who spilled out of the holt in complete confusion. It seemed as though there was a division, indicated by bickering and much quarrelling. The oldest remaining brother (after Ela and Alamanth) was apparently the cause of the trouble, or at least the center of the situation.

"Mother!" cried one of Roath's younger sisters, "Jeyla pulled my tail!"

"No I did not!" Jeyla shot back. He turned to face his concerned mother, whose paws were folded in a no-nonsense stance.

"Jeyla, tell me what happened," she commanded sternly.

The lad's ears flattened nervously, his paws held up pleadingly.

"I really didn't pull her tail! Honest! We were simply just playing tag. Ask anyone here!"

Their mother glanced at each one of her children. Indeed, each of them bobbed their heads in agreement.

"It's true!" one piped in. "Jeyla was 'it,' and he caught her by the tail while she was running."

The Matriarch glance at her daughter whose tail had been pulled: "Drian, is this true?"

The young lass' eyes fell, nodding. "Aye, mother."

"Then what was all the fuss for?"

Drian looked back up at her mother, indignant. "Because it hurt!"

The Matriarch smiled, bending down to where her eyes were level with her daughter's. "You must have been running rather fast, then, weren't you?"

Drian's expression had changed from one of indignance to a fit of giggles. "If you'd seen how scary Jeyla looked, you'd have run all the way fast, too!"

Her mother gave her a quick nod towards Jeyla. "Then why don't you say you're sorry for getting angry at your brother?"

Drian bobbed her head obediently. "Aye, Mother!"

The little lass turned and bounced over in front of Jeyla. "I'm sorry, Brother. Will you forgive me?"

It took a long moment of pouting at hazel eyes begging at him before Jeyla began to smile, and then laugh.

"Aye, I forgive you!"

Brother and sister hugged. Their mother smiled

approvingly.

Out of the blue, one of the young syannetts glanced to the mountain to the north, and asked, "Why did Father go up there?"

The Matriarch's gaze followed the pointing paw. "Your Father goes up the Mountain every autumn, when the leaves begin to fall. He stays up there for a time, usually ten days, before returning home."

"But why?" repeated the little one.

Roath's eyes widened in realization, and turned to her mother. "They haven't heard of the Beginning, yet."

The syanness nodded with a sigh, sending a glance over the small sets of staring eyes watching her expectantly. "Aye, I know. I wanted to wait until the time was right. I believe it is now."

With a sweep of her paw, she gestured all of her progeny, the youngest of which was born last spring, into the mouth of the holt's entrance.

"Come, my little ones. It is time that I tell you why your father returns to the Mountain."

Moments later found the syans gathering in a semicircle facing the Matriarch. She sat in the center of the main entrance room as she began to tell them of the very first day of time, of which she was a witness. While she was busy speaking, her eldest daughter was drawing the curtains closed across the few windows, and lighting several candles in various places; all this was to provide the appropriate environment for her younger siblings to most effectively visualize what they were hearing.

"Many seasons ago, before there were seasons, your father and I lived as the only syans of this world, placed here by the Creator to live. However, this world was far different, covered with such beauty that I cannot even begin to describe. We lived in that paradise with many other species, including the Otters, Hares, and Squirrels. There were all kinds of fruit to eat in one big place. We even talked with the Creator's offspring many a time. It's hard to say how long we lived there, but everyone we knew remembers the day it all ended." She shook her head sadly.

"What happened?" asked Jeyla. "What caused it all to change?"

The Matriarch shook her head in confession. "I don't entirely know. One day, while we were walking about, the ground beneath our paws began to shake back and forth, causing us to lose our balance and fall. While we slowly recovered from the shock, the sky above changed. Before, there had been a most brilliant twinkling of stars covering the canopy of night; but afterward, and ever since, the stars became dim. We noticed that a similar change had come upon the sun and the moon. We had expected the quaking of the land to stop at once, but it was a long while before it had finally ceased, perhaps hours; it is hard to say, as days were quite different then.

"After it was over, we immediately went to the Otters to see how they'd fared the unexpected change. The four of us looked about, and noticed that something else was missing; but we could never put our paws on it, save that our sense of balance was heavily affected for many days after. I think what disappeared so suddenly was the paradise, but your Father still feels to this day that it was more. We did, however, see that something else came in place of whatever it was."

"What was it?" asked an older kit. His mother stroked his mane.

"A distant mountain had appeared that was not there before. Everyone was surprised to say the least, but no one seemed to want to go near it, not even us at first; but as the days became the length we're used to, your father began to have dreams of it. That lasted several seasons before we finally came to this place to search out why it seemed to want us to come. We settled here, not too far from the Mountain's base, for I did not wish to go up. But your father still insisted that it was still calling to him; and so he went on his own for a few days. Not too much later after he'd returned, Ela and Roath were born. He told me that he wanted to take Ela up to the summit when he was old enough, but never said why. Every time I asked, he would become distant and quiet. I never knew what happened, but I never went up the Mountain to find out."

"Why?" asked Drian. "I want to be high up on top with Father. Why don't you like the Mountain?"

The Matriarch opened her mouth to answer, but stopped. She really didn't have an actual reason not to go to the summit with her mate. It wasn't as though that anything had really held her back; she just hadn't truly put much thought into going. Perhaps it had been because she never felt the same call her mate did, and reasoned that she was not meant to go. The Matriarch glanced out through the single round window facing towards the Mountain, and sighed.

"I do not know," was all she could think to say.

Shortly after midday, the three male syans made an unexpected halt. They had been trekking along when Kahren's paw flew up, signaling his sons behind him to stop. The lads' looks changed to ones of concern as their father quietly began to sniff the air, his pointed ears rotating on either side of his mane.

"What is it, Father?" Alam asked in a hushed whisper. "Is there danger nearby?"

Kahren slowly raised a paw to his lips, indicating silence. Scanning the surrounding trees on both sides of the path, he spotted a slight movement amongst some bushes. He motioned his sons to stay in place, and bounded with a deft leap over and vanished into the leafy shrubs. Seconds later, a male voice sounded out, too high to be the deep bass of their father.

"Owoww! Leggo, you big bully!"

Kahren and a young otter came rolling out onto the stony path, locked in a playful wrestle. The otter, though he was bigger and stronger than his syan opponent, was quickly pinned with his face against a sizable rock, paws held behind his back.

"Ow," he grunted, squealing a few unintelligible things that Ela suspected were directed at his father, "I say! Can't an otter get a fair fight up in the mountains?"

"That's why you otters stay near water, where you have the terrain advantage." Kahren grinned, releasing the otter's paws. He stepped back, helping his defeated opponent up to his paws. Both heartily embraced, the twain clearly old friends.

"Hahaha! How've you been, Jallin? It's been a while since I laid eyes on your fat muzzle. How are your father and mother these days? Well, I presume?"

Without even waiting for an answer, Kahren immediately set about introducing his sons to his friend, giving the otter Jallin a clap on the back.

"Ela, Alamanth, this here is Jallin, a good old mate of mine! He's the firstborn otter of this world," he said with a wink towards his eldest son. "He's not much younger than you, Ela. I don't suppose you know him, since I met him while I was traveling alone. Why don't you both greet him?"

"Hello," Alam said, bowing respectfully.

Ela, mildly distracted in deep thought, gave a polite nod. "How do you do?"

Rubbing his sore wrists from the wrestle, Jallin nodded back toward the two lads. "Doin' fine, thank ye. Going back up the mountain, are we, Kahren?"

The older syan cocked his head in response. "Aye, every autumn as usual, Jallin. Now, what brings you back to this country? Your father took the lot of you out west three summers ago, right?"

Jallin looked at him in surprise. "Three summers? Has it really been that long already?

Kahren nodded with a chuckle. "Indeed, it has been three summers, I think. You father took you all so you'd have a proper wetland holt to call home."

Jallin nodded. "Aye, that he did. He found a very fine place out west, alright, just four day's journey on paw for an otter, if we made it quick. The hollows actually live not far beyond there by water travel, in a cypress forest swamp. Or at least that's where they hold their ceremonies and whatnot."

"Indeed, indeed," Kahren quickly cut in. "Now why are you here?"

Jallin nodded. "Well... I actually came to find you.

Figuring you'd be here along this trail, I decided to wait here until you either came up or down... And here you are!" He spread his paws wide.

Kahren grinned. "Come to see an old mate, have you? I would have figured that this unexpected visit would indicate a special event of sorts. Were it just a visit to see how we were doing, you'd have waited until I returned to the holt, but I sense that there's another reason. And, I get the impression that you have something exciting to tell me?"

Being more obvious than not, Jallin was practically brimming over and trembling with joyous news: "My mate has given birth to twins!"

Kahren's eyes widened, sending an amused side glance to Ela. "So, you're a father now, are you? Congratulations! Are they sons or daughters, or both?"

Jallin smiled proudly, puffing up his barrellike chest. "A strong son and a beautiful little daughter. They've taken after their mother and me: when you see them it'll be obvious they got their mother's looks, and you can guess where they got their charm." He motioned a paw to his furry chest, twitching his eyebrows.

Ela leaned in towards his brother. "Oi, he's certainly

full of it, isn't 'e?" He muttered with a grin, low enough that the otter would miss the comment. However, their father caught the remark, flashing a grin and shaking his head.

"Well, Ela, when are you going to give me and your mother some grandkits? We're just dying to see a third generation of syans crawling around the holt. Why, Jallin's younger than you, and he's already got some progeny!"

Jallin the Otter made a grimace. "Ahh, don't push 'im too hard, Kahren. My Father says you syans age slower than us. Don't worry, I'm sure you'll get another generation soon. Speaking of which, how many children have you got yourself?"

The older syan glanced at his two sons. "Including these lads, my mate's given me twenty and all."

Jallin's jaw hit the ground in shock. "A-a score, you say?" he stammered. "But there's only eight in *my* generation so far! H-how?"

Kahren cocked his head, still grinning all the while. "I'm sure your father meant to say that syans age *differently,* not necessarily more slowly. But aye, I also figure I'll get more little 'uns soon, along with those grandkits."

He sent a narrow glance to Ela, who only stared back and forth between Kahren and Jallin without so much as a word. He was completely silent, and apparently distracted. His father turned back to Jallin.

"Right, then! I believe you've come to invite us to see your newborns, am I right?"

"Somewhat. I'm actually bringing my family here to this area. I didn't think it would be right to take you over all that distance. Ye don't mind, do ye?"

Kahren shook his head. "*I* don't. My mate is the one you might have the harder time persuading, considering as she has a score and two stomachs to feed."

"Two more won't make much of a difference, I would think," responded the otter. "Even then, my mate Jolah and I can fend for ourselves. We could even catch some fish for a contribution. I understand you syans would like that, right?"

The older syan looked down over the treetops towards his home. "I'm sure she would appreciate that. However, you'll have to excuse me and my sons for the time being; we've got a Mountain to climb."

All four glanced up at the remaining portion of the

rocky trail; along the sides of the winding incline, the pine trees began to thin out, providing little shelter from any elements that might head their way. The last leg of the trail was going to be quite a challenge indeed.

Jallin turned and began making his way down the stony path. "Well then, don't let me keep you too much longer. I won't want you to miss that special event on my account!" he called back as he departed.

Kahren and his two sons looked at the steep climb before them. Alam, who up to that point had remained silent, asked, "Special event? What special event was Jallin talking about?"

The older syan rubbed his paws together, beginning to make his way up the trail again. "It would take longer to explain it than we've time for before it begins. And if we miss it, the storm will get us first."

Alam and Ela exchanged glances. It was obvious to the younger of the two that his elder brother knew nothing of any storm. Both quickly took off after their father, not wanting to wait around to find out.

<u>Chapter 4</u>

That very afternoon sun beat down upon the brows of two young gara lads facing one another in combat. Both stood in a field of tall grass that came up to at least their knees, though most of it for leagues around went up to their waists. The only shade offered in the region could be found in a nearby grove of trees that served as their clan's home.

The elder coolly eyed his opponent, whose forehead was damp with perspiration. The younger's teeth clenched in frustration, the knuckles of his paw becoming sore from being wrapped so tightly around his weapon, a hardwood staff. Both were so armed, garbed in deep blue kilts traditionally worn by their kind. They, like all gara, had a compact slender build, pale fur, enlarged skulls, and pointed ears that stuck out from either side of their head. Their eyes were usually dark, but the pale blue eyes possessed by the elder combatant were an unusual feature. It was these eyes that watched and with ease anticipated the every move of his junior opponent, thus blocking and deftly sidestepping at the blink of an eye. Moments had passed since the last blow had been swung.

"What's the matter, Malyth?" the pale-eyed gara taunted his younger sibling. "Are you out of deceitful tricks to pull?"

Malyth, as he was called, glanced through narrowed eyes. He had lost patience long ago, his frustration and anger rising.

"Well, it's all fine for you to say, all-seeing Seer!" He spat, finally throwing down his staff. Swift as lightning, his opponent swung his staff behind one leg, catching Malyth off guard. Before he could react, the younger gara was flat on his back on the long grass, the wind knocked from him. He gasped for breath as the Seer stood back and began to pace around him, using his staff for walking, placed twixt them. He spoke with a throaty voice as Malyth wondered why he was getting yet another lecture.

"It is unwise, brother, to rid yourself of your one defense in the middle of combat. Were Father here, he would be ashamed of your so easily surrendering."

Malyth sneered. "Surrendering? Or deciding that this is all a waste of my time?" He sat up, still glowering sulkily.

"Your Seeric abilities allow you to all too easily anticipate my maneuvers. You already know where and when I'm going to strike. Why even bother attacking?"

The Seer leaned in close. "Because I can only move so quickly. Just because I'll know where you'll strike doesn't mean I can block all assaults. Why do you think I never struck you down until you tossed aside your staff? Because, I know that you're fast enough to block me. That's why I focused just on defense. Now, brother, get up, and don't give in so easily this time, or ever. You're better than that, especially with your gift of tricks. Now, up!"

After doing a bit more practice, they stopped for a rest, turning toward the shaded area. Malyth was still bitter, but was force to bite his tongue. There was never winning any argument with his brother. But he always had the rest of the tribe to take his irritation on, so indirectly that they never knew who was responsible. Except, of course, the Seer always did.

As the gara brothers made their way into the grove of trees nearby, the grass became shorter, most of the soil nutrients here drawn into the towering trunks instead. Dominantly fruit trees, the gara clan never wanted for food. With plentiful resources, their most productive time was spent creating new combinations of taste.

In the center of the trees, the firepit was kept by several of the pale-furred creatures at any given time. Though it was not uncommon for gara to get into arguments over the pettiest things, this literal and cultural center of food usually reaped the most cooperation the members of their race ever got.

Except when a new recipe went sour.

One male gara, the other three accompanying him female, raised a ladle from the small cauldron over the fire. Taking a sip, he nodded his approval to his mate.

"This stew's a winner!"

His mate beamed at the rare statement of approval. The other females turned from their respective cutting up apples and pineapples for fruit salads, eager to take a swig themselves. Any success took priority over potential ones, especially with food. But of course, the two grabbed the ladle from the male simultaneously, and started tugging it back and forth to see who would get to try it next.

"*I'm* older. I get seniority privileges!"

"*I'm* prettier. I should get to try it, you always get it first!"

The latter remark cut the first to the core. She turned on the male, her grip on the ladle unwavering.

"Who would *you* say is prettier?"

A third female, his mate, was suddenly standing between the male and the squabbling pair. "That's not a fair question, you should ask someone else! You already know what answer he'll give." She turned and winked slowly at him.

Malyth suddenly appeared on the scene, bearing a new ladle. "Relax, you lot are supposed to be getting supper for the rest of us, not spending all your time fighting. You both can try it at the same time. This isn't that difficult."

The male cook gave a look of relief to his rescuer,

silently mouthing, "Thank you."

Malyth sent a quick nod back. "I expect a really good meal from for you four, Seer and I just came back from practice."

"Oh?" the male cook perked his ears. "How'd that go?"

Malyth shrugged. "Oh, you know how it is. He sees everything I've got, but I have strength and speed on my side."

The younger female winked at Malyth. "I'm sure it must be exhausting spending all that time in the sun."

He cocked his head. "It's not much. I do need to get cleaned up, though. If you'll excuse me..." He took the ladle from the two females, and dipped them both, one after the other, into the cauldron. Malyth presented the original back to the young lass while giving the new one to the older female. The latter grunted her thanks and the young male took his leave.

He got about a score of paces before the fighting began. Not even turning back, he continued toward the spring, where the Seer already stood, dabbing his face with a towel. He sent a narrow glance to Malyth.

"One of these days, I would actually like to taste one

of the successful recipes."

The younger gara smirked. "You always do."

The pale eyes didn't waver. "*Without* any of your modification. Whether you realize it or not, the stuff you put on that new ladle is going to permeate the entire cauldron. We're all going to get a dose of what you gave *her*." He motioned to the older female through the trees, who was at the moment pushing the female responsible for making the stew. Malyth only heard snatches of the argument, something about picking a mate with the worst possible taste buds. He shrugged and took the towel from the Seer.

"Get her to leave the younger lass alone, and I can arrange to spare the next new meal."

Seer shook his head, silently thinking, *The one Time you one something nice for anyone, and of course it would be her.*

Ela could hear Alam struggling below him on the rock face. All three syans were climbing up one after the other, taking clutch of any pawholds that yielded promising grip. Having travelled it numerous times, Kahren was well in the lead. However, he went deliberately slow to vocally guide the younger of his two sons, whose efforts were giving as much success as when the younger lad had first started on the trail. However, he quickly remembered to follow after his elder brother, as with earlier.

"Alamanth, are you pressuring your pawpads along the rough edges of the rock?" his father asked. "Our kind was made for scaling steep cliff faces such as this one, so you must know how it is done!"

"Aye, Father!" Alam called back. "Don't you remember last summer when you took us fishing at the creek near the river? You showed us how it was all done then."

Ela grinned down over his shoulder cockily. "Wasn't that the time you slipped and stunned a fish when you landed on it? I couldn't stop laughing at the squealing noise you made! I've never seen anyone so startled like that afore!"

Alam glared back up. "That wasn't funny at all! I thought that fish was going to stun me back with its tail when it recovered. How'd you expect me to react?"

"Enough of that talk, now." Their father had called down as he finally pulled himself over the final ledge. He stood up and surveyed the surrounding terrain. "Once you make it up here, we're done climbing entirely. The trail goes up a little more, and we'll be there. We'll rest awhile before we continue walking, though."

The elder syan shielded his eyes with a paw as he glanced toward the sun's position in the sky. "However," he added, "You might want to hurry. Sunset is an hour away, and we've got to get there before twilight begins to set in if we want to see the whole thing. Come on, now!"

However, Ela was still thinking of Alam's fish incident and began to snicker, barely stopping himself before his brother's ears rotated up.

"I heard that!" Alam exclaimed.

The sun began to dip low in the horizon, casting lengthening shadows across the land. There was a stillness in the air, as though the Earth and sky both dared not to whisper, more solemn than ominous. The darkening heavens seemed to glow with an unearthly light to all beholding eyes that searched, gazing upward for the inevitable event nearly upon them.

Many hollows watched from the trees of the forest, many hanging by their long winding tails from the limbs, others resting in vantage points in the leafy foliage, for those in the aspen trees; a few chose instead to perch in pines, preferring less of their view blocked by the thin needles to the aspens' wide leaves. Most of them were gathered to areas where the perching trees were either taller, or afforded the proper branches.

The greatest number of those Strange Ones, as they were commonly called, had resorted to the wide upswinging boughs of the most immense sarcras tree; they were gathered for the coming-of-age ceremony to take place that night.

Boom! Boom! Boom! Boom!

The sudden bellow of a drum pounded the air for half of the entire surrounding league to hear. Scores of pointed ears twitched with anticipation, all eyes upon the center of the celebration: Salari.

Boom! Boom! Boom! Boom!

And so it continued, the ongoing beat, sounding in a rhythm of four. The young male hollow stood nobly and resolutely in the crown of the sarcras tree, his gaze fixed and undeterred toward the setting of the sun. As was tradition, one of his age was to watch the horizon three degrees off from the fiery orb until it completed its descent below the horizon; nothing was to distract him.

Boom! Boom! Boom! Boom!

The sole purpose of the tradition was to prepare the young ones to transition into adulthood. Complete focus was requisite. Distraction could easily lead to death in a young world where dangers were not entirely known. All they knew was that anything could happen.

Boom! Boom! Boom! Boom!

At long last, the sun and Earth met. The disk of the sun began to vanish, the flaming edges extending a final leap before disappearing entirely. The drums beat faster and faster, until the air was nearly thrumming with the rapid beat.

BR-R-R-R-R-R-R-R-R-Rrrrumm! Ba-Bum!

The pounding ceased with a final two beats the instant the sun was obscured completely. Letting out a sigh of relax, Salari allowed his gaze to fall to the ground below, no sunset to be fixated upon. He turned as his father began the next portion of the ceremony. Moaren stood upon a high branch where all could behold him. He stooped over bent, his head sweeping slowly back and forth as he glanced upon his tribe.

The chieftain suddenly threw back his head, ritually

letting out a spine-chilling noise resembling a hissing shriek blended with the cry of a wolf. Immediately, he was joined one by one by the other hollows until all present were too emitting from the depths of their throat the high-pitched call; all except Salari. He was to remain silent until spoken to.

The lead hollow of the drums ended the cry by throwing his weight down upon his instrument.

BOOOOMMM!!!

All fell silent instantly. The Tribal Chieftain waited for all eyes to be fixed upon him—as many other hollows were summoned by the collective cry—before he spoke, loud enough for all to hear.

"Tonight," he called, "Is distinct out of all nights in the year, of all seasons. Every autumn, we wait for the event coming just moments from now. And..." he paused, glancing at his son, "When one of our kind approaches the age of adulthood, they must be ready for survival on their own, as soon there will be a great too many of us to lead as one tribe. Tonight, I call all of you to recognize my son as a born leader! In times of crisis, he has shown wisdom beyond his age, such as when the plague of serpents began to sweep the land twelve seasons ago. He helped all to safety at his own risk! Most of you are witnesses, are you not?"

There was a collective round of hisses and shrieks of agreement.

"Hisssshhhaaahhh!"

Their chieftain waited upon the branch until the noise died down to continue.

"And what of the sinking marshes? Did he not risk his own life to save others who would have otherwise died a horrible demise of suffocation, buried in mud?"

"Hisssshhhaaahhh!"

"Very well, then! There are numerous other events all of us can cite, but for shortage of time, they need not be mentioned. He has shown physical prowess, loyalty, and obedience! And all other things needed for a strong leader!"

There was another round of agreement. Moaren the Chieftain continued.

"Now, every leader needs a name to distinguish himself from all others. Salari!"

The young hollow came forward as he was bidden. Moaren leapt from his perch overhead, twirling about and landing deftly on all fours beside his son. He stood upright proudly. He then stepped back a pace ceremonially. Each looked straight into the other's eyes.

"Salari, I Moaren, Chieftain of this tribe, and as your father, hereby give unto you a name; one that signifies you as a leader and a protector to your kinsbeasts; and also, a charge that you shall always focus your mind with honor, and that you shall always be true to another; and lastly, that you shall take upon yourself the official responsibility to protect your tribe, even at the cost of your own life, and never betray the trust of those close to you. Do you accept all these things that shall accompany your name?"

Salari replied solemnly: "Yes, I do accept this duty."

Moaren nodded. "Salari, as you are now an appointed leader, you shall now be bestowed a new title: from henceforth, you shall be called, Salari the Warrior."

Waiting until the sudden cheering died down, Moaren riveted his eyes back toward his son. "You shall bear this new title and responsibility with support from your Tribe." He turned to face the remainder of the gathered hollows.

"Tomorrow, in celebration of the Star Event nigh to

occur, my son shall treat you all to a skillful display of flying upon his okara. I recommend you all come, for it is a feat you won't wish to miss. Now, all rise to the treetops! It is beginning!"

Referring to the imminent celestial display, his words were confirmed as the stars appeared in the darkening skies, the last throes of twilight dissolving. Out of the constellations that normally ruled the night, a single star that was usually invisible to the eye glowed brighter than all the rest. After shining brilliantly like this for a few moments, it winked out, only to be replaced by another bright star just degrees away from where the first had appeared. Soon, more of these strange but fascinating stars appeared in other locations across the sky, taking on an almost hexagonal pattern. The sky seemed to take on a brightness of its own, the normal points of distant light being dimmed out by comparison. It was truly glorious indeed.

The hollows were not the only ones privy to the miraculous occurrence. At the peak of the mount, the three male syans were also witnesses. However, having a much wider view of sky and land from their vantage point, they could see more fully the brilliant display than the distant hollows.

The transcendent array of beauty like a glittering jewelbox spilled, that caused the color and luminosity of the stars to amplify, had begun just as Alamanth had stopped yet again for a breath. He was as the night before, hunched over, his lungs sucking in air with effort, only to exhale more quickly. Though Kahren did not seem to be trying to push his younger, less-experienced son too hard, Ela could see impatience and urgency furrowing on his father's brow. Around them, the stony and now-barren ground, for their altitude was too high for much to grow, was lit from above, allowing them to see all of their surroundings almost as though morning had come in a cascade of rainbow hues.

Ela glanced toward his father, meeting his gaze as the young syan lad motioned for permission to continue on. Knowing that his son knew where the trail ended, Kahren reluctantly nodded as he tried to aid Alamanth upright to stand. However, the latter was weak from the climb, not having had much real experience before with the physical strain, especially in the thinner air of higher altitudes. He stumbled every few paces, and Kahren decided that his son really needed to rest. He and Alamanth made their way over the pebbles to a nearby rock slab that made a convenient sitting spot. The young lad looked up to his father, still trying to regain steady control of his breath. By this time, Ela had already long since gone ahead, and was out of sight.

"Father," Alam wheezed, taking a glance to the twinkling band above, "Why must things change?"

The elder syan's wise eyes became puzzled. "How do you mean?"

He took another deep breath. "Well, last night, when I asked about that dream I had, you wouldn't answer. Ela and I could tell that you were pretending to be asleep. Also, this morning when I found you meditating, you had fear in your countenance. Ela looked the same way when he woke me, but he was trying to cover it. It seems as though both of you have had the same dream I've had."

Kahren fell silent. Hunching down, his expression darkened, only obscured by a brief sorrowful smile.

"Alamanthea, while I am proud of how your skills of observation have developed, I am, unfortunately, concerned about the whole situation with the dream. There's no point in denying it now. It would be dishonorable for me to lie about it when the Creator wishes the twain of us to know."

Alam finally slowed his breathing, though his limbs were shaky and weak, his paws sore from the day's journey. "What about Ela? Doesn't he know as well?" he asked.

Kahren was till solemn, staring at a red star that outshone all the others for a moment before winking out with a flitter of sparkles that spread outward. "Aye, it would seem that he does."

There was a moment's pause. "Father, what does it all mean?"

Both looked upward. The elder syan sighed. "I don't know. I really don't know."

The Seer stood silently between two aspen trees growing at a slight angle away from one another, watching a rocky hilltop a treelength from his position. Sunset gone by nearly two hours now, he waited where he was at until the moment was right.

The gara, sensing that the time was now around the corner, raised a paw and waved it, motioning three creatures behind him to follow. Forward they went: the Seer, along with his mate, and also his brother Malyth, and a young female gara that Malyth was courting, the same that he had assisted earlier during the stew squabble. The four made their way carefully up the worn stones of the hill, all of them heading for the summit. Unlike for the hollows and syans many leagues distant, this sky was silent and still, no celestial display to be seen. Consequently, the younger of the male garas was distracted stealing glances at his lady friend as she looked to the stars.

Suddenly, Malyth jabbed his footpaw hard on a sharp, jagged edge. Momentarily forgetting that the pretty young lass was present, he shrieked in pain, falling to his backside.

"Yowch!"

Tenderly clutching his injured footpaw, the male gara fought back tears of pain. His female companion bent down to inspect it.

"Malyth, are you alright? Let me see your wound."

At first, he resisted, still holding his paw. However,

the faint starlight glinting off her large dark eyes melted his stubbornness, if not some of his pride. He reluctantly showed the damaged paw, releasing his hold.

Dark blood oozed slowly from the pad. The young lass, named Yase, inspected the wound carefully. Taking a kerchief, she cleaned the injury gently, removing some shards and specks of stone that had apparently flaked off and imbedded into Malyth's paw. He clenched his jaw, trying not to let Yase see his discomfort. The Seer's mate stood nearby, watching.

"There, there, it's not that bad," Yase whispered softly. Having some practice with medicine, she took a strip of cloth and wrapped it around until his paw was bound tightly to stop the flow of blood. She smiled at him.

"We can treat that later. Come, we don't want to keep your bother waiting too long." She extended her paw and helped him up. Limping along, she supported him with her shoulder. Malyth winced with every step. Aware of how easily he became annoyed at feeling helpless, she spoke softly and soothingly.

"Don't worry. I'll help you up to the top. It's not too far, now."

The Seer's mate followed along after them. The Seer, seeming as though he had completely ignored his younger brother misstepping, was already upon the hilltop, stargazing. He paid no heed to the padding pawsteps coming up from behind. Yase helped Malyth to sit down, the young male unable to remain standing for long.

The elevation at which they stood was nearly level with the surrounding treetops. A chilly autumn breeze swept in from the north, chilling their fur. Each of them shuddered, shivering briefly until the light wind was past. Yase sat down beside Malyth, glancing into his eyes, their conversation silent.

The Seer's mate, named Jalo-in, came to his side closely for warmth. Addressing him by his real name, she nuzzled his eartip. "Aka, why exactly are we out here tonight? You seem to be intent for this particular time. What is going on?"

His unusually pale eyes searched the dark velvet skies. He raised his paw, motioning for her to keep her voice down. Jalo-in noticed her mate's gaze darted back and forth ever so slightly.

"Aka, what is it?" she whispered. "What are you

doing?”

"Star Reading,” came the hushed response.

“Star reading? What’s that?”

“Listening to the stories of the stars.” His paw rose again, sweeping to the expanse above, though his gaze focused on a reddish star that was so dim, that it was barely visible. “Each point of light you see is another sun. You know that many of my visions come from what our Sun sees, yes?”

Jalo-in nodded her understanding.

“Well, all stars see the area of space around them. Not only that, but they speak to one another, sharing their each and every story. Star reading is hearing the tales being told.”

The Seer’s mate paused a long moment to listen. Only silence met her ears. She shook her head, somewhat doubtful.

“I don’t hear anything.”

“Not hearing with your ears, Beloved,” he lightly reproved. “I see that few will ever possess the gift. The hearing is in my mind. I hear the stars speak in my head.”

“What do the stars, say, Aka?” she asked, whispering

as she sent a glance to the courting couple nearby.

He shook his head. "It was they that called us here. I still do not know why."

The gara couple stood together, side-by-side, watching the wide dark expanse filled with twinkling stars.

Chapter 5

Upon the mountaintop, as well as in the various other surrounding regions of the land, strange events apart from the starry display were about to occur. The first anomaly, a spirit having a shining appearance, glided through the sky like a night eagle; it appeared as just an odd energy radiating off of a dimming star. It stopped in midair for an instant, searching the Earth half a league below for its target. It was here for a very specific assignment.

Spotting the dark mountaintop, it saw the mouth of a cave, knowing instantly that it was where its target creature was. It could see also the areas where its similarly-appearanced companions would go. Each of these apparitions or spirits, looking exactly like celestial beings should with their almost blinding visage, were all to find specific creatures that were able to perform a great and rare task, one that only a few mortal beings could do. The Creator had instructed these spirits that very specific creatures were to do it.

This first spirit, having found its mark, honed in like a predator to its prey. There was no time to waste.

Ela hurried along until he reached the very end of the trail, right at the entrance to a shallow cave. This small cavern was just spacious enough that it could serve as a shelter from a storm or gusty wind if such things were to ever come. Fortunately, there was no sign of the dreaded storm that the syan lad's father had mentioned. He glanced around the cave's now-familiar interior.

When he had been here the previous autumn, as well as all other times he'd come with his father over the last six autumns, Ela had either been so exhausted and tired from the journey, or had been asleep the instant he rested, that he missed the wonderful events that had taken place in this small cavern. His father, though stern at some times and compassionately wise other times, would never tell him exactly what had occurred; rather, Ela was getting the impression that if he could not remain conscious enough to hear or see what had happened, then he would never find out.

He was surprised to see how sinewy he'd grown since four seasons ago; he was able to take this journey with greater strength than he'd ever experienced thus far in his life. Then again, perhaps all the slowing up for his brother had made it all less strenuous for him this time. The syan lad liked the former idea better.

Before these thoughts of self-absorption had too much longer to take root, Ela was brought back to reality as he noticed an odd light beginning to fill the stony enclosement. He turned.

There, standing real as life in the back at the spot furthest from the mouth of the cave, and much to Ela's astonishment, was the glowing figure of a syan about his age. It looked at him with a serious but calm expression. Almost instinctively, rather than letting his surprise turn to fear, Ela felt trust and love filling his frame. The lad knew that he had no need to be frightened. The spirit creature spoke.

"Ela."

Hearing his name being uttered, he let out a sigh of wonderment. Respectfully, he knelt, knowing that his radiant visitor must surely be sent from the Creator. He only knew it wasn't the Creator Himself, as Ela had been taught that the influence of such a visit was beyond his ability to remain standing.

The spirit raised his paw, motioning Ela to get back up. He continued speaking.

"Ela," he repeated in a profound yet still voice, "You shall not bow nor kneel to me, for I am a special servant just as yourself."

The syan lad froze, both humbled and taken aback.

"What special servant?" he asked. "I'm just a syan, like yourself; what makes me distinctive? I mean, aside from the fact that I have a body?"

The spirit raised his head slightly. "Ela, you are not ordinary. All are different in their own way, but your soul is not of syannic origin as the rest are. You soul has been changed in form so that you could have this body. You were once of the Creator's own."

Ela tried to process all this. He glanced around anxiously as though random rocks offered answers. The spirit syan spoke again.

"Ela, this is new information to take in; this I know. But nonetheless, you have been given a task to do. That is why I am here. I am to tell you what the Creator wants you to do, and to give unto you the gift to accomplish it."

The syan lad eyed this apparent messenger. "Who are you?" he asked. He listened intently for a response, his ears now confidently perked.

"My name is Iven," the spirit responded. "Know this, we shall meet again. Later we shall speak more concerning who *I* am. Ela, you are not the only one that shall be given the task this night. Four other young males shall be visited by spirits like me, and they shall also receive the gift. The reason you are first is that you specifically are called to be the Preservant leader of them."

At this point, all Ela could do was stare at Iven the Spirit, openmouthed and dumbstruck. Although he had been hoping for so long to witness something happen in this cave, he was not quite prepared for this. Here he was, being told that a great task from the Creator was about to be done, and he was to lead other lads to do it?

The spirit Iven watched Ela before him, waiting a

moment for the young syan to contemplate the revelations.

Surprisingly, for reasons he just could not place his paw on, the news of this assignment seemed to make sense, more quickly than he'd anticipated. He had expected it to take some time to sink in, at least the part regarding his soul's origins. It was not that he was a commanding individual or even a leader, as he might have expected offspring of the Creator to be; but he had always been different from others in a way that he couldn't quite put his paw on. Nonetheless, he felt the beginnings of a great burden of responsibility that would come in grander measure later on, no doubt.

"Ela, do not fear, neither allow worry to trouble you. The Creator's first Son shall be your Master. Whatever strength, whatever power is needed for any part of this task, shall be given by the gift which the Master provides."

The young syan blinked a couple of moments, unsure of what to say. He had always been told by his mother and father that the Creator was all-knowing and possessed great love for His offspring, though they were another species entirely. However, as hard as it seemed to believe what this spirit was saying, the syan lad still had that burning feeling in his heart that what he was told was indeed the truth. He couldn't think of any other way to explain it to himself.

Having turned away for a brief moment to consider the rush of these and other thoughts, Ela faced Iven with a stance of determination, his face hopeful and unafraid.

"If this is what the Creator wants me to do, then I shall do it," he stated bravely. "Now, just so I understand: what are the task and the Gift?"

Though Salari the Warrior had witnessed many times the annual stellar display, it never ceased to amaze him, placing his mind in the deepest state of awe. Even as a young one, he felt his mind drawn to those stars that brightened, danced, and faded in an almost complex but orderly pattern.

The young hollow Warrior faced east, but occasionally glanced to the south. Had he or any other hollow glanced to the north, where the least star activity was taking place, they would have seen another spirit similar to Iven descending towards the sarcras tree where they were gathered. Being the furthest hollow on that side of the gathering, there was no physical creature to Salari's back to witness the apparition as it approached him through the air. This spirit, having the form of a hollow, alighted upon the limb just behind Salari. However, unlike his companion Iven, he held to the nature of the species of his form, being unseen the instant he wrapped his over-lengthened tail around a sturdy nearby branch. He moved in behind the young Warrior, none of the mesmerized spectators of the stars even sensing his presence.

This hollow spirit, unlike his syan counterpart, hid his light. This would be the one time he and Salari would meet or encounter one another. While Iven had promised to visit Ela again, this hollow and the Warrior would not do the same. The spirit looked at the silhouette of Salari sadly, and placed both paws on the lad's back. The spirit hesitated, marveling at what he felt. He knew that hollows had two hearts instead of one, and could touch the double heartbeat of Salari. *Is this what that feels like?* The spirit wondered to himself.

Shaking the distraction from his mind, the hollow spirit instantly bestowed the Gift into the twin hearts of Salari the Warrior. To the perspective of all around him, the lad issued the slightest groan as he suddenly collapsed, and the imperceptible spirit took his leave.

"Take care, little one," the apparition muttered, turning to ascend back to the sky. He leapt up and away, gliding over the treetops, allowing the shroud to dissolve that hid him from beholder's eyes. He stole a final glance back to the towering sarcras tree that stood like a solitary guard over the forest.

"Soon to be my home," he sighed to no one in particular.

Chapter 6

While the gara wondered why they were there so late into the night, the answer to their collective question looked from high above upon the tiny hilltop far below. There were two spirits, both gara. The male spirit led his mate downward, honing in upon the mortals to be called to the tremendous task ahead. They glided on an unseen breeze that spiraled downward in a series of eddies, lowering gracefully from the sky.

There they are, the female thought. *All four of them. Is the Seer truly among them?*

Yes, her mate thought back. *He is the one that led them there. He is awaiting our arrival.*

Does he know why he is meeting us? She thought.

No. Come, we must hurry, he nodded his head downward. The hill was now two treelengths distant.

The male spirit gara was first to appear, his mate just heartbeats behind him. The radiance that shone from their luminescent figures lit up the nearby trees, drawing instantly the attention of the quad of gara. Malyth, in complete surprise, tried to jump upright, only to collapse with an agonized gasp of pain. The other three, even the Seer, stood dumbstruck at this appearance. The male spirit glanced over them, his eyes resting on the injured lad. He spoke.

"None of your need fear. Malyth, what have you done to your paw? For what injury is it bound?"

Wise enough to want not to cross this heavenly being, Malyth replied straightforwardly. "Some stone cut me. It's just a little scratch. Nothing to be bothered with."

"Then why do you not stand with the lass you love? I sense a great deal of fear in you. Such a state does not become one who works so heavily with the heart above that of their mind."

Though Malyth suddenly realized how worried he

had been about seeming unimpressive and helpless in front of Yase, he was getting annoyed with this spirit revealing his closed thoughts of his in front of her and the others.

"Now, wait a moment!" he cried indignant. "Who are you to say how I feel about anything? Who said that I was afraid?"

"Only fools feel no fear," the divine being countered. "Bravery and courage belong to those who will not allow their fear to overpower them. If you wish to show that you are not a fool, *and* have courage, then go to her side."

The statement struck Malyth to the core. He knew that if he remained sitting, he would be showing fear toward the pain in his footpaw that would result from standing. If he stood, he would have to swallow his pride in the process by obeying the divine directive. There was no middle ground.

Five sets of eyes watched him as he hesitated, then used his good remaining footpaw to push himself up as he leaned his weight on his forepaws.

To his astonishment, no jolt of pain shot through his body as he stood on his bound-up paw. Yase and Jalo-in both gasped open-mouthed at this. Malyth had expected to be made to look like a fool, but instead his paw was completely healed, not a single lingering sensation that the cut had ever existed. He quickly bent down to untie the strip of cloth, a close inspection revealing the pad and binding to be normal, no blood to be found. In shock, the usually temperamental gara lad went to Yase's side. All four looked up at the spirits standing in the air over them.

"Malyth, you are the first to have used the Gift, having just healed your own footpaw. All four of you this night obtain the Gift."

Bewildered, the Seer asked, "Gift? What Gift?"

The male spirit gara looked down sternly upon Aka the Seer. "You see all of Time, but know not this Gift? All of you little ones are being commissioned this night for a challenging task. A task that shall begin soon, and spanning all Time until the End. The Gift is power to repel death until your task is complete. You likewise possess resistance and strength against sickness, disease, and injury."

"What is the task?" asked Yase.

The male spirit stepped back in the air, his mate

taking his place. She began to speak, her voice softer in tone than his.

"We should now introduce ourselves. I am Arfelacas, and my mate is Tokardis. He has answered and told you what the Gift is. I shall now tell you more about the task itself.

"You four, as well as others, are to become Preservants. This means that over the course of Time, you are to keep watch over and lead various species to live and survive until Time Ends. There is a coming event that will threaten the lives of many creatures. The remnant will be divided from one another. The Preservants are to care for each division until they are to return together. The task will take a very long Time, and cannot be passed on from generation to generation; it must be done by the same who start it. This is the reason the Creator gives you this rare Gift."

Arfelacas then stood back, allowing her mate to come forward again. He was serious.

"You all have been given the Gift in part. Until each of you near death for the first time, it shall not be given in full. Now," he cautioned, "Never are any of you to misuse the Gift for selfish purposes. It has safeguards that will cause severe consequences for such abuse of power. Your Preservant leader is now himself being commissioned to this task. You all are to follow his direction, lest you stray down the wrong path. The Creator's Son Himself will commune with your leader to guide and direct your efforts. Never betray this commission. The Course of Time is dependent on you. Go; and may fortune smile upon each of you. Farewell."

As Tokardis the Spirit's instruction came to a close, he and his mate Arfelacas began to fade from view. The light and radiance retreated back to just their glowing forms, their figures dimming until they were gone.

The quad stood dumbstruck, staring openmouthed into the sky. They waited like this for several moments upon the stony hilltop, the light patches of grass swaying in the breeze that began to pick up from the previously still air. Malyth was the first to recover from the shock. He turned and faced the others.

"Well now, that doesn't happen too often. Shall we head home? It's getting a little chilly out here."

<u>Chapter 7</u>

Having given instruction and information regarding the task and Gift, much like the gara spirits had, Iven faced Ela for a short moment to allow the young syan to absorb what he'd been told before he continued.

"Do you understand why this calling exists? Does its full magnitude weigh on you?"

Ela nodded uncertainly. "So this group of Preservants—you called them—is supposed to stay alive forever?"

"Until the End of Time."

The young syan stroked his whiskers. "But where will these separated groups be divided to? And what is the event that shall make a division necessary?"

"These shall be revealed in due time. For now, know that you will be guided by the Creator's Son through me and other mediums. He shall reveal at each stage of your task what is to be done. Know that each Preservant called has a unique set of gifts that they will use to aid you. Never forget that they are fellow Immortalims that will look to you to for direction. They are your greatest sources of help. Until those times of task and revelation arrive, be content with and use the knowledge which has been made known to you."

Ela was unsure of what to say. His thoughts raced wildly, his emotion mixed between excitement and anxiety over the impending assignment before him. He looked down, rubbing his chin, the feelings rushing through him betrayed by his elevated and uneven breathing.

"This is all real." Though intended otherwise, it was more of a statement than a question. Iven only watched as Ela continued, and began pacing.

"My goodness," the lad said under his breath. "Me... I am to lead others to save lives for all Time? Given power against death itself... and each of us gifted with various other abilities all the while?" Stopping and turning back to the spirit syan, Ela asked, "Who are the others? Are any of them syans as well as us? What about my family? Will they join me?"

Iven glanced past him to the mouth of the cave just paces away. "Aye. Your brother is to be a Preservant also. Here he comes."

Ela turned around to see the silhouette of two dark figures approaching the cave's entrance. Behind them, the stars were still in the process of performing their display. As Ela's father and younger brother made their way in, their faces were illuminated by the light of Iven's brilliant form. Kahren and Alamanth squinted as their eyes adjusted. The latter raised a shielding paw.

"Father, what is it? What's happening here?" he asked, shocked and amazed. Never before had he imagined such a thing as a visitation by a spirit, despite Kahren's account from the night before. Their father knelt humbly before Iven, both of his sons positioned beside him.

"O spirit, are you the one that I have communed with for these many seasons? I can now see your face. I have never known your visage to be of my species in any past visitation, for it was hidden from me. Is it you?"

His mouth gaped, awed by Iven's presence. However, the spirit syan turned his attention to the youngest of the three syans.

"Alamanth."

The lad lowered his shading paw from over his eyes. "Aye?"

Motioning with a glance toward Ela, Iven gave a final instruction for that night.

"Alamanthea, you are now to take the name Artitan, for that is the name by which you shall be known for all Time; also, listen carefully to what Ela tells you. He shall explain all. In return, you are to help him be humble. Neither of you can afford arrogance or pride in your task. Your older brother is now leader of the Preservants. Farewell."

In the same manner that the gara spirits had departed, so went Iven. But as he disappeared from view as they watched, the light in the shallow cavern didn't go with him; if anything, the cave got brighter and brighter. All three syans were startled to see that the source of the light was Alam, now called Artitan. He looked down at himself, his figure seemingly more radiant than Iven had been. He looked up into the staring gaze of his father.

"What is happening?" he asked. Ela, having just conversed with Iven, knew what was coming upon his younger brother. He stepped forward.

"He's giving Alam, er Artitan, the Gift," Ela explained. "The power to resist death to the End of Time."

Salari had no recollection of losing consciousness, nor did he have any idea as to what had caused him to collapse. All he did know is that one moment he had been standing on his perch in the gnarly limbs of the sarcras tree, the next he was slowly regaining consciousness in brightly-lit surroundings. As his vision began to clear, he could see a small figure stooped over him; judging by the angle, he realized that he must have been laying on a table or cot of the likes. Everything around him was still blurry and spinning; he could, however, distinguish the voice belonging to an uncle of his in the background.

"I just don't understand," he stated repeatedly. "First the lad completes his part of the ceremony impeccably with ease, and then an hour later inexplicably faints and falls all the way to the ground. On top of it all, by the time we get there to see what has happened, there's no sign whatsoever of any injury! No bruises, cuts, scrapes, or broken limbs. I just don't understand it."

As Salari the Warrior heard his father's reply, the creature bent over beside him turned away for a single (of his double) heartbeat, and then turned back. All at once his vision cleared. Standing over him on his right was a pretty young hollow that he recognized, but had only seen briefly several times before.

"Neither do I," replied Moaren, the hollow tribe's chieftain trying not to furrow his brow. "However, there must be a logical explanation. We can continue to ask around and see if any hollow saw what happened."

"That's the problem," his brother replied. "If we inquire around too much, everyone will get jittery if it looks like it might happen again. We'd best keep it to a select few that already know about the incident."

"A select few?" Moaren scoffed. "If by that you mean just about everyone in the tribe, no worries about the word spreading to too many others!" He hissed in annoyance.

Salari, however, paid little to no attention to the conversation in the background; instead, he was absorbed by the beauty of the female hollow, who was busy inspecting his left paw for damage from the fall. Suddenly, she noticed he was awake, and released his paw. She leaned back and turned her head.

"Chief Moaren! He's awake!" she called.

As the two elders cut short their discussion and approached the tableside, a glance passed between Salari and the young lass. He was so awestruck by the pretty eyes, that it took his father calling his name several times before the profound trance between them was broken.

"Salari! How are you? Are you alright?" Moaren asked in concern.

The young Warrior suddenly snapped back into reality. He tried to sit up, somewhat dazed, but his uncle, who stood to his left, held him down.

"Not so fast, Warrior. You're hardly supposed to be in any condition to exert yourself in the slightest. Now, what exactly happened? What is the last thing you remember before you lost consciousness?"

"Sorry?" he asked, bewildered that he could not recall.

"Before you fainted?" his uncle offered, thinking Salari had misunderstood him.

"No," the Warrior began, "I meant... never mind. What did happen? What am I doing here?"

The three creatures standing over him fell into silence. Salari took time to take stock of his surroundings. They four were in a familiar white-stone cave, bright sunlight pouring in through the mouth. Salari suddenly remembered that this cavern was not too far from the main sarcras tree.

Moaren shrugged and sighed. "I honestly don't know how to explain it fully myself. You were there hunkered down in your perch. After the first hour of the stars dancing in the heavens, you stood up. Just moments later, someone yelled, and we all saw you fall to the ground, completely limp. Everyone thought the fall had killed you at first. Yet miraculously, here you are alive and unharmed. Jeen here was the first to get to you." He motioned to the hollow lass, who only stared somewhat worriedly at him, and then introduced herself.

"Hello, I'm Jeen, the Healer," she took a slight bow respectfully.

"I'm Salari, the Warrior," he replied with a nod. "Pleased to meet you, I'm sure."

"Likewise." Turning to Chief Moaren, she said,

"Well, I don't see anything wrong with him. Either he's got a tough hide, or a miraculously rapid ability to heal. Whatever it is, it saves me a lot of work. I'd say he's fit to go." She motioned him to rise from the table.

However, Moaren was a little skeptical. "Son, are you sure you're fit to ride your okara?"

Salari shot up quickly with haste. "What hour is it? The display is to happen an hour afore noon!"

"Warrior, worry not," his uncle began. "*When* it is to happen is not nearly as important as it actually happening. Besides, you still have more than an hour to go even then. That should be sufficient time to call your okara Jehleen, should it not?"

Salari however was already on his way out of the cave. He stole a final brief glance at Jeen, and then departed without another word. The three remaining hollows exchanged looks, completely baffled at the strange series of events that had occurred in the last twelve hours.

Chapter 8

Despite the events of the previous night, there was a huge turnout of hollows gathered to see the flying display of Salari and Jehleen. As before, all were perched upon branches and limbs of the great sarcras tree, many using the ripe fruit for their morning meal. Many others were napping contentedly with their tails wrapped around their hefty perches, having obtained little rest from the night before.

Salari was concealed in the roots of the hidden entrance. He looked out, leaning his weight on a paw resting on the gnarly bark. The sight of the dying turf outside caused a faint sensation of sorrow within. Slightly bewildered as to why he was feeling this way, he squatted down, stooping over a small flower wilting in a pose of near-death.

The petals were nearly brown and flaky. Salari the Warrior remembered that this kind was his mother's favorite. Normally, during the spring, this flower was brilliant shade of white with streaks of lavender wisped across its delicate surface, but now it lay in the first throes of the oncoming winter. He ran his paw gently over one edge admiringly, only to watch as it disintegrated into flakes, leaving a pathetic, uninviting stump of a head. He pulled his paw back quickly.

"Poor little thing," a voice behind him said.

Salari's head whipped about, still in a crouching position. It was Jeen! Somehow, she had sneaked up behind him without his notice. It always amused Salari the Warrior how stealthy members of his species were, especially to one another. He stood up courteously.

"Winter's coming," he replied. Then, he remarked, "It kind of makes one hate that season, doesn't it?" He motioned to the deathlike flower.

She shook her head. "Perhaps at first glance. But, that's the beauty of nature. Winter is little more than sleep." Bending down to the pathetic-looking plant, she said, "It's called a summershade. It is actually a good thing for winter to do this to it."

"How?" he asked, puzzled.

"Parts of the plant are useful for medicine. It can only be harvested before the frost sets in. Were summer to continue on forever, the summershade could never shed its seeds. Eventually it would die without another generation to follow after it. Likewise, it is healthy for other flowers and shrubbery. The deathlike state of winter allows for the rebirth of spring."

Salari the Warrior looked out of the sarcras tree roots towards the now-autumn sky. "I never thought about it that way," he said, stroking his whiskers pensive.

Suddenly, there was a collective chorus of hisses emanating from above. Salari stepped paces forward, noting the sun's position in relation to the zenith. It was time. He glanced toward Jeen, his head nodding upward.

"You might want to join them up there," he said, grinning. "You wouldn't want to miss the show, would you?"

She turned and quickly clambered her way up, but not without first batting her pretty eyes at him.

"Of course not, my honorable Warrior."

His narrow cheeks flushed red, and he ducked out, hoping that no one above was watching.

Jehleen the Okara did see it all. He hovered on a warm updraft high in the deep blue expanse of the sky. Despite the flying creature's normally playful and mischievous behavior, he was getting a wave of dread filling his slender frame that he just couldn't shake off. The feeling that something terrible was going to happen was all that his mind was able to focus on.

Nevertheless, the high-pitched shrill that signaled from below for his arrival to the clearing he could not ignore. He leaned over and shot down in a spiraling arc, letting out a majestic cry:

"AAAAAYYYYAAAAAAHHHRRR!"

With the typical manner of gust and flurry of his species, Jehleen glided to a graceful halt upon the dying grass. He swiveled about on all fours towards the massive sarcras, waiting only a short moment as Salari the Hollow Warrior made his way to the okara's side. Salari stroked his mount's neck soothingly, clearly sensing the internal agitation that was building.

"There, there, it's all right," Salari whispered in the okara's flattened ear. "What's the matter? There's nothing to worry about."

Immortalim: The Call

It had been many long seasons ago when Jehleen first met the hollows. His first winter was horrific and devastating, harsh storms ravaging much of the land, leaving trees, shrubbery, and fields coated in the cruel grip of ice. Anything left exposed to the merciless onslaught of the stinging blizzard froze in cold agony. Many creatures had been relatively well prepared, however, and by huddling deep in their homes and burrows, they kept clear of the wailing dirge that swept the countryside in an unstoppable wave of chilling destruction.

And Jehleen, the young okara, was caught in it.

Grounded and unable to fly without great effort and making no progress against the gale, he was left helpless to brave the storm on paw. Left alone, as he was then of the age when okara usually began seeking time away from gatherings of their kind to discover their own visionary identity, he had no one but himself to keep him pushing onward. Where to go, he did not know; all the okara did know is that he had lost all sense of direction and location. His situation looked bleak.

Even his youthful energy was insufficient to keep him going very long. He was completely alone, helpless, and cold. That, and the lack of aged wisdom and experience of his elders left him with little hope for survival for much longer. At long last, his strength completely failed him. He collapsed in numb exhaustion, his consciousness fading into utter white oblivion.

The next thing he could recall was coming to in a warm firelit cavern where a family of hollows that had rescued him was brushing the last of the chilling snow off of his wingtips. He waited until they finished and stood back before he arose and stretched himself in the inviting stone cavern.

Amid the brunt of painful wincing as he waited for the numbness to dissipate, he noticed a young hollow about his age watching him intently with awe. Okara had always been known for their ability to sense future events, and even with the young Jehleen, it was no exception. He knew that instant that this hollow lad had a great destiny in store.

The two had since become the best of friends. In the days, weeks, and seasons that followed, Salari first watched the okara fly high, then he eventually mounted, then learned to maneuver. After the time they spent, they soon synchronized, and fell into a rhythm to operate as though they were one creature. It was for this reason that Salari and Jehleen had done so well while Moaren had watched them. The young Warrior had decided not to tell his father quite yet that they'd had much practice already.

Still trembling from the wave of dread, Jehleen knelt down as Salari the Warrior mounted him. The okara stood and padded around the misshapen clearing until they were at the far end towards the tight cluster of trees surrounding the open grass.

Pausing for a brief moment, the mount and his rider glanced to the sky.

Suddenly the okara collapsed, falling on his side. Salari sensed it just in time to swing aside, so that Jehleen's weight would not pin him down. There was a collective gasp and whispers from the onlooking hollows. Jeen quickly scaled down the gnarly sarcras limbs and darted over, sensing her healing skills were needed.

The male okara, feigning his sudden passing out into unconsciousness, opened a sly eye, watching carefully.

As soon as she was at Jehleen's side, she checked to see that he was breathing.

"What happened?" she asked Salari, passing a glance

of concern. He could only shrug dumbfounded, unsure how to react.

"I have absolutely no clue. One moment he was alright, then he just fell. You don't suppose this is what happened to me, do you?"

Jehleen unexpectedly rose as quickly as he had fallen. One wing scooped up Salari onto the okara's back as a remount maneuver they once developed. The other wing did likewise with Jeen. She let out a yelp of surprise as she was placed right behind the Warrior Hollow.

"What's going on?" she cried in alarm.

Salari had just put the pieces together. He gave his mount a playful smack on the shoulder with the back of his paw.

"You big rascal, you set this up!"

Pretending to ignore the accusation with a slight grin, the okara broke into a run. Salari's whippy tail looped around Jehleen's slender waist as Jeen grabbed tightly in fright to the Warrior, so as not to fall off.

"What's going on?" she repeated.

"Just go with it." He shook his head, bemused at his best friend's deceitfulness. He guessed that Jehleen had seen their conversation from earlier.

The okara spread his wings wide, catching enough air to lift straight up. Having seen everything from a distance, the hollows in the sparse foliage of the sarcras tree let out some rasping cheers mixed with snickering at Jehleen's antic. Okara just had that kind of sense of humor.

They three rose high into the sky. Jehleen banked left, spiraling in loops, progressing higher with each crest. Climbing until each hollow far below looked as though they were mere specks, the okara suddenly dove into a barrel roll. Jeen cried, holding tightly to Salari, who only hunkered down to minimize the air pelting him. Just before reaching the ground, Jehleen spread his wings wide, jerking into a level glide. Jeen panted as Salari patted her grasping paws reassuringly before he braced for the okara to start another round or maneuvers.

After several more brief but intense series of aerobics, it seemed as though something came over Jehleen. He swerved northward in the air without warning. Salari leaned to look at his friend's expression, the okara's eyes staring blankly ahead.

"Jehleen? Enough of that."

Despite the Warrior's tone, the okara held his course.

Salari tugged at his neck fur, but the larger head stared on straight.

"Jehleen, this isn't funny! Head back to the gathering!"

The mount continued on, not showing any intention of stopping. Realization dawned on both Salari and Jeen that something was very wrong. In a single exchanged glance, they knew they were helpless to do anything about it.

Chapter 9

Still trying to recover from the overpowering awe of the night before, Kahren and his sons were making their way back down the pebbled trail that they had hiked two days previous. The descent was easier by far in comparison to their ascension, though there were moments where it took some effort not to descend too rapidly. It was now late afternoon; yet, despite the amount of time that had transpired since they began making their way home, Artitan was still trying to make sense of what had happened. As he tried to obtain answers from Ela, their father kept pushing them to move quickly, chiding out of alarmed concern.

"Hurry, my lads. Believe me, we don't want to get caught in this storm. It's going to be bad."

Artitan inquired from behind him. "What do you mean? Is that why we're not staying the full time?"

Without even looking, the Patriarch nodded to the left.

"Look east. That, and the air has been too still. There's always a calm before the storm."

They paused for a glance. Blackened clouds were slowly massing their way across the sky, ominous figures that towered high above the horizon. The brothers could make out lightning forking in the heavy underbelly, occasionally lashing out upon the Earth with such fury that it sent chills down the manes and spines of Ela and Artitan just from looking. They could already hear the faint rumble of the accompanying thunder. The storm was indeed fast approaching.

The syan lads quickly followed after their father; not a few heartbeats later, the solemnity of the moment wore off.

"I'm not sure if I understand," began Alam for what seemed the hundredth time. "*What* exactly did this Iven give me?"

"It's actually for both of us, or so he said," corrected Ela, pausing in place. "It really didn't look as though he had given me anything. I find that *awfully* strange, considering as *I'm* supposed to be the leader here."

"It *is* strange, but can we discuss it when we return to the holt?" Their father Kahren sent a troubled glance to the side, undoubtedly at the prospect of facing the unnaturally powerful force of the storm bearing down on them. "Or keep moving as you talk. I'm sorry if I seem impatient, but I just want us to safety as soon as is possible before we get caught. Do you both understand?"

"Aye."

"Aye."

"Good. Hurry! You may talk if you feel you must, just don't slow up. We can stop for a rest when we reach the creek."

The brothers suddenly fell silent. With the prospect instilled in their minds, their paws quickened. Nothing right then sounded better than a rest, however brief, by the creek.

At last, Jehleen the Okara showed signs of landing. For much of the day, he had glided high on warm air rising from below, too high for the young hollows to have any chance of dismounting safely in midair. Northward they had continued, ever since the okara had seemed to have lost his mind. They too could see the approaching storm from the east, and Salari several times had tried to steer his friend to turn back, but to no avail. The clouds were now close enough that both Salari and Jeen saw they would be caught in the furious gale long afore they could fly to the safety of their forest grove. The young Warrior knew now that there was absolutely nothing he could do but try to see where Jehleen was taking them.

As their altitude decreased, Salari's Warrior instinct caused him to take note of what their new surroundings would be. The rapidly rising treetops of this new forest weren't as dark as they were used to, the foliage less dense. Ahead, a mountain stood solidly in their path like a stoic megalith ready to block the closing storm, offering protection to the leeward west side. Before them lay a sparsely-wooded grassy clearing, in which Jehleen was steering to land.

Not knowing whether his friend was in his true right mind quite yet, he glanced over his shoulder to see that Jeen was very much frightened. He knew that whatever happened, whatever the outcome, the young Healer had to stay safe.

"Try to stay calm, Jeen," he tried to comfort her. "Hold on tightly, so you don't fall off when we land."

Her small paws obediently squeezed harder on his waist.

The okara began to flap his wings to slow down. He leaned right, spiraling downward, the ground flying up at them. Jehleen lowered all four paws, galloping at first until they came to a complete stop. Salari motioned for Jeen to let go, and then dismounted. He held her paw as she shakily did likewise.

"Where are we?" she shivered nervously.

Eyeing their surroundings with a tactful glance, he replied, "I don't know. Jehleen and I never came here before. Jehleen, what have you done?"

The okara stared blankly ahead, clearly in a trance. Salari waved his paw before his friend's eyes, but he was still unresponsive. Looking more closely, the Warrior sensed the okara was having a nightmare of a vision. He turned to Jeen, helpless.

"Have you ever dealt with anything like this as a Healer?" he asked anxiously.

Before she could answer, Jehleen began to shudder violently, and collapsed. Jeen was immediately at the okara's side for the second time that day.

"He's fainted!" she exclaimed, glancing twixt the two. "What are we going to do now?"

Salari only shrugged, eying the dark clouds now beginning to loom over them. A faint breeze started to pick up, the power increasing by the moment. The bare tree branches began to sway and click together, the air filled with the sudden rustling chorus. It seemed as though their chances for returning home quickly were now very slim.

Jeen turned her attention away from her winged patient, staring up at the young Warrior.

"Go find a place to stay the night," she advised, her voice taking a barely detectable tone of an unearthly authority. "I'll stay with him."

As he turned to do as bidden, he asked, "Will you be alright?"

"Yes." There was no mistaking the urgency in her statement. He quickly hurried away towards the trees, trying not to let the low-hanging branches catch his haldris.

Kahren, Ela, and Artitan hurried, now more desperate to return to the holt than stop at the creek as they had originally thought. The first wave of the storm was nearly upon them, the wind slapping furiously against their pelts. Young Artitan risked a glance up at the clouds, and witnessed the furious wrath of destruction descending upon them.

"Ela!" he called out over the howl of the rush of air. "I hope our Gift protects us from this!"

"What?" Ela turned back to hear his brother's response, misstepping at the edge of the cliff overlooking the creek below. All three were suddenly knocked off their paws by a massive gust. Their father quickly regained his balance while Alam stumbled several paces; however, Ela was not so lucky.

"FATHER!"

He was catapulted clear off the ledge by the force of the wind, plummeting out into space.

"NO!" yelled Kahren as he helplessly watched his eldest son hit the shallow waters below.

The Hollow Warrior Salari had just risen to the crest of a nearby hill when he heard the cry, just barely over the wind, followed by a faint sickening thud. In alarm, he quickly darted towards the commotion, watching from behind the cover of a fir tree to make sure that he was not running straight into danger. Seeing all was clear, he made his way hurriedly to the water banks.

What he saw caused his hearts to sink with pity. A young creature, a lad a little older than he, lay stunned in the rocky edge of the creek. At first, the Warrior hesitated, unsure whether he should go get Jeen to come to help, but some inner feeling caused Salari to instead bend down over him.

Quickly taking in the features of foxlike ears, mane, otterlike body and hazel-grey fur, the hollow realized that he was gazing upon a syan for the very first time. He'd heard of them, but had never actually seen one.

The syan groaned and weakly turned. He squinted and realized Salari was standing over him. Confused by the haldris that hid much of the hollow's frame, he croaked, "Please... help me."

With a slight motion from him, Salari the Warrior saw what the problem was: a sharp, pointed rock had stabbed into the syan's side, causing him considerable amounts of pain. He gasped.

"One moment, syan, there's someone nearby who can help. I'm not qualified..."

The syan only weakly looked, his eyes struggling to stay open. "Please, help."

He suddenly winced. Not willing to leave the syan's side should anything happen in his absence, the first idea that popped into his head was to remove the stone. His mind raced. Another option, one Salari thought unwise, was to carry the dying creature to Jeen. The Warrior opted for his first impulse.

Not wanting to prolong the discomfort, his paw took hold of the stone. The syan was now on the verge of losing consciousness, his eyes distant. Salari gritted his teeth, and pulled.

The stone removed easily enough, and the Warrior at first thought all would turn out well. Instead, to his horror, the trickling waters around his footpaws ran red nearly instantly with blood. Salari froze in panic, the bloodied stone held in the air. Except for the rushing wind whipping his fur about, he was still, his breathing broken by the occasional gasping sob at what he had just done. He could only stare at the young syan before him that lay dying and helpless.

His trance was broken by the sound of pawpads running toward him. He turned and saw just downstream two other syans fast approaching. The older one, in the lead, held an outstretched paw toward the body in the stream, his voice just audible over the surging noise.

"Ela!"

Trembling, Salari dropped the stone upon the other rocks and fled from the scene, his wet footpaws trailing red prints a short ways on the brown grass and loose rubble. The Hollow Warrior ran for all he was worth, darting into the trees. After covering a considerable distance, he stopped and broke down in tears and leaned against the trunk of a cedar tree. Shame and remorse coursed through him. Thoughts taunted him relentlessly as the full realization of what had just happened dawned upon him.

Why didn't I take him to Jeen? He wondered over and over again, his face buried in his paws, sobbing heavily that he had made such a mistake. *Why did I just leave him there?*

Amid his weeping, he was unaware that he was not alone. Above him in the bare swinging foliage of a nearby oak, the translucent form of a spirit hollow stood. This hollow had a special connection to the young creature below, sent by the first to watch. He eyed Salari sadly, wanting so desperately to speak to the young Warrior, but knew it was not yet time to make an appearance. But it would be soon enough.

High above, the clouds obscured most of the sky, the full force of the storm just beginning.

Chapter 10

Fat raindrops began to fall, leaving dark spots that dotted dry stones and the bark of trees. Chaotic ripples marked the surface of the creek at the foot of the cliff. The red-dyed water was nearly dissipated, washed along downstream.

Just on the banks of the creek were the three syans. Kahren had just fashioned a bandage to slow the loss of Ela's blood. His eldest son was now completely unconscious and unresponsive to any of his surroundings, his breathing quick and ragged. His pallor was pale, his appearance disheveled and gaunt. His father shook his head, sadly as he knelt over him. The vivid nightmares that many a night had plagued him were now coming true.

Artitan stood nearby. "Father, is he alive?" he asked, worriedly

Kahren sighed. "Thankfully, but just barely. Go, tell your mother what has happened. I'll be along shortly with Ela. Be quick about it!"

His younger son obediently shot off towards the holt as fast as his paws would carry him, despite the distance that remained for him to cover.

Kahren slowly turned his eyes back toward the limp form of Ela, when something caught the corner of his sharp vision. He quickly glanced back. To a syan so widely travelled, there was no mistaking it. He bent down for closer inspection, hoping it wasn't so. Sure enough, it was hollow pawprints.

Made of Ela's blood.

Not even noticing that his exhaustion from the last two days had vanished, Artitan rushed across the dying turf towards the sarcras tree of the holt. Long moments had passed in what seemed a surreal few heartbeats between the creek and his home, his heart rising to his throat. The young syan fought on through the force of the wind, knowing his brother's life depended on it.

"Mother!" he cried desperately, pushing his way through the front entrance door. "Mother, come quick! Ela's hurt!"

She stood up quickly from her old chair. "Alamanthea, slow down! Now, tell me what happened? What's all the fuss about? Where's your father?"

Artitan swallowed hard. "Ela fell. He's been wounded bad. Father's on his way with him now."

Extreme worry crossed her features. She glanced past her son, who turned in time to see Kahren bearing the half-dead body of his elder brother. The younger members of the syan family began to emerge from their bedrooms down a long hall. When Roath, Ela's twin, entered and took in the sight of her twin, her eyes grew wide.

"Father, what's happened to Ela?" Jeyla asked, the first to break the dread-filled silence.

"Why isn't he moving?" Drian chimed in, her eyes wide.

Kahren cocked his head urgently towards the young ones. "Alamanth, take them to another room. Distract them for now. Children, go with him, and do as he says. Save your questions for later. Go!"

Despite the staring eyes, they obediently followed their elder brother away. Roath was motioned over. The syanness Matriarch had only stood speechless the whole time. Kahren knew exactly what she was about to say. He only knelt down, setting their son upon the earthen floor gently, suffering terrible déjà vu as he struggled not to make eye contact with his mate.

Her motherly instinct kicking in. she quickly knelt down at his side.

"Kahren," she cried, "What happened?"

The syan Patriarch flinched. "There was an accident. He was close to the cliff near the creek when the storm struck. It seems as though he fell onto a shard of stone that stabbed his side."

"*Seems?*" asked Roath. "How did you know then that it was a stone?"

"The wound itself was jagged," came the grunted reply. "However, which stone remains in question, because by the time I arrived, there was no indication of where it went. It was simply gone."

A hushed silence fell upon all three.

The deathly quiet that had filled the room was interrupted by the sudden entrance of another creature into the holt at the main entrance. Shaking his fur clear of rainwater, he blinked at the syans staring up at him from the dark interior. It was Jallin!

"Sorry about me bargin' in here, but the storm is makin' quite the mess, and that doesn't bode well with getting a load of fish to transport, let alone get a few bites worth anything," he began. The otter quickly saw Ela. "Hullo, what's all this?"

Kahren gave a quick nod for him to enter. Jallin turned for a heartbeat, nodding to a creature behind him. The otter came in from the storm, followed closely by his mate Jolah, who carried two tiny kits protectively from the rain. She too saw the comatose form of Ela, and gasped. "What happened?"

After yet another round of explanation went out from Kahren, Jolah suggested that they start a fire to warm the now-chilling interior. Her mate Jallin and Kahren together got a blaze roaring to life in the mantle in short order as Jolah and the syannic Matriarch set about trying to help Ela recover quickly.

Roath gulped. "What will we do to help him recover

from the loss of blood?"

Her mother shook her head. "The best I think we can do is preventing any further loss. He'll either recover... or..."

Jolah patted her shoulder. "Here, let's not worry about the worst-case scenario. Let's put our heads together once we've got him properly tied up, and see what we can figure out in the way of speedy recovery. Sound fair?"

The syanness Matriarch nodded with a sigh of relief. "Thank you."

Salari hurried his way through the sparse trees of the forest. Neither the rain nor the wind seemed to bother him at that moment. All that mattered was for him to make his return to Jeen and Jehleen. He had found an abandoned den dug into the roots of an oak tree that stood out above its smaller companions.

He couldn't go back to the syans to explain what had happened. Right now, there was a storm raging, the elements venting fury upon any creature left exposed to Mother Nature's inexplicable vengeance. He guessed that by now the syans had already returned to their dwelling. With his limited knowledge of the area and even the species, he was left with little indication of where to even begin to look.

Salari quickly continued onward towards the clearing where he had left his okara and the Healer, not wanting them to be left another moment in the storm.

When Jehleen had pulled the stunt earlier as a ruse to have both Salari and Jeen mount him, Moaren was hardly surprised, given the okara species' incredible foresight. He had known for a long time that his son and the Healer wer practically meant for one another. Despite their different occupations and talents, he knew that their combined wisdom would provide the ultimate leader and his mate.

All of which was exactly why he felt initial concern at their sudden and unexpected departure, and their absence over the last several hours. But he knew both Warrior and Healer could take care of themselves, more especially each other. What he didn't know, however, was that their departure was not their doing. Believing the circumstances to be different, he was chuckling inwardly over their little stunt of flying away, expecting their return in the next few hours. He was sure that in any case, they would be getting to know one another a lot better than they had before today. How they had not run into each other that much, Moaren didn't know; but even if their flying off was responsible for putting them into danger, the hollow chieftain at the very least was glad that he had brought them together outside of the infirmary, the one place Salari almost never went near.

"Are you sure they'll be alright?" Moaren's mate asked for the third time now. Both rested on a perch high on the sarcras tree of their woods, watching over their domain. They sat with their backs to the bark of a thick, hefty limb supporting their branch.

"Of course they will," the Chieftain smiled proudly. "It wouldn't surprise me if they've already found a new dwelling place for part of the tribe to live. Salari knows his way around here."

"But what about those clouds? Isn't that the last place we saw them going?" She pointed to a dark, hazy patch on the northeastern horizon. It looked somewhat angry and menacing. However, Moaren eyed it with disinterest, the mass seemed too far away to be of any concern. He only shook his head, smiling confidently towards his mate.

"Don't worry yourself, Beloved. I'm sure they haven't wandered *that* far. I don't think they're anywhere near there."

Caught in the very midst of the storm, Jeen and a very weak Jehleen fought their way through the blustering bellows in a desperate attempt to reach the cover of the trees. The okara had barely regained consciousness, his paws trembling as he struggled through the very thick of the blasting onslaught. He held one wing protectively over the hollow maid, shielding her from most of the chilling sleet that had begun a persistent barrage of pattering upon the clearing. The trees were not too far off now.

The okara remembered very vividly that winter storm of long ago in which he had been stranded. Then, he had been younger and more energetic. Now, he was an adult, and struggling to protect a lass of the species that had saved him. Together, both pushed on to brave the storm, barely reaching the trees as Salari suddenly appeared to view.

"Follow me!" he cried. "I've found a place of shelter not too far away. Hurry, I think the worst of the storm is yet to come. It's approaching fast!"

As if to confirm his statement, not a moment later they were suddenly hit with a massive blast of wind. Salari protectively took hold of Jeen's paw in one of his own, shielding his eyes with the other. By now, both of the young hollows' haldrises were flapping about, catching and snagging on outstretched tree branches that hung low to the ground. The elements howled wildly, whole trees beginning to sway back and forth. They pushed onward, plunging through the torrents of fur-chilling rain.

At long last, they reached the oak tree the Warrior had earlier discovered, in whose roots lay the old dwelling down the hole. Salari led them to the entrance.

"In here!" he motioned with his free paw. The Warrior gently helped the Healer over a root forming the threshold. Once she was within the protection, he glanced towards his okara.

He breathed with a doubtful hiss through his fangs. "It's going to be a bit of a squeeze."

As he started past, Jehleen weakly gave Salari a look

of guilt. The Warrior normally would have asked what the matter was, but he suspected that he already knew the answer: the okara had likely seen in a vision what Salari had just done; he was now thinking his stunt and loss of control that brought them here had caused it. The hollow began to stroke his mount's neck comfortingly with a sad look.

"It's all right, Jehleen. What's done is done. Come, we must get us all in shelter. Up and over, Jehleen. There, that wasn't that bad, was it?"

Having assisted Jehleen over the small space, both of them drenched and soaked wet from the downpour, Salari made his way into the dark, dry tunnel in the roots of the immense oak tree, followed closely by his mount.

"Now what?" asked Jeen.

Salari eyed the tight interior narrowly. "First, check that we're safe down here. It doesn't smell like anything's lived here for a while, but the rain could be playing with my nose a bit."

Jeen cocked her eyebrows. "Then the second thing to do would be to dry off. I don't think getting tossed down a raging river could have gotten me quite this soaked."

As if in agreement, Jehleen shook himself, spaying

water everywhere. The hollows raised their paws to shield their faces, but to little avail.

Salari flicked drops aside off his paws. "Agreed. I don't have a change in garb, unfortunately. I don't suppose you fared any better with your medicine bag?"

Jeen shook her head. Salari pursed his lips.

"I can wait then to air-dry."

Jeen shook her head. "It's dark enough that whether you keep your garb on or not won't make a difference. I won't see a thing."

Salari twitched uncomfortably. "Well... I haven't exactly spent a lot of time around a maid, so..."

The Healer rolled her eyes. "I've treated wounds enough on tribal members. Besides, it's the only way to get yourself dry without risking a cold or pneumonia. If it makes you feel any better, I can go explore a corridor down that way a bit, since I need to let my garb dry as well. Deal?"

Salari nodded, relieved. The Warrior just didn't feel right exposing himself in front of a female like that.

After Jeen's padding faded down the corridor and Salari pulled off his haldris, he laid his clothing over an overhanging root to allow it breathing space. Turning, he met the gaze of Jehleen. The okara gave him a narrow stare.

Salari raised his paws defensively. "Hey, we've known each other since we were young. It's not like you'd think weirdly of me."

Jehleen shook his head and motioned to his own back with a sweep of his triangular head. Salari chuckled.

"Oh, that's what you meant. No, it's okay that *you* never wear anything, you're used to it, the rest of us are used to it, and besides, it would get in your way during flight. For me, I'm just accustomed to having this on like anyone else once I got old enough. I just haven't ever been down to bare fur in front of other hollows in a while, that's all."

Jehleen shrugged, making a few muffled squawks. Salari rolled his eyes and looked more closely at some of the walls of the abandoned dwelling.

"Odd... for a home so crudely made, I'm surprised that there aren't things like claw marks or bedding made of fur. But these dimples here on the floor in the corner look like they could have been sleeping areas. Hullo, what's that, Jehleen?"

The okara motioned his friend over, and began

drawing in the dirt with a stick held between his teeth. In the dim illumination of the lightning strikes flashing through the entrance, Salari watched with fascination as the winged creature shaped some sort of rodent-looking form. The Warrior met Jehleen's gaze as the latter dropped the stick aside and presented the quick but moderately detailed sketch.

"You've seen one of these before?"

Jehleen nodded.

"So you have seen them, but you've never been out this far, have you?"

The okara shook his head, and then flared his nostrils. Salari nodded.

"Oh, so you can smell that they lived here? You can remember their scent from meeting them a while back?"

The okara nodded.

"That's impressive memory. So, I can tell that these things haven't lived here if some time... if they came back, would they get aggressive over us borrowing the place like Father would?"

Jehleen shook his head, and then took a paw and placed it gently on Salari's head. He pulled back and held the paw at the young male hollow's height, and then dropped it to almost a third. The okara nodded toward the drawing. Salari understood.

"They're not aggressive, and they're only that tall compared to me. Too bad you can't tell me the name of them."

The okara retrieved the stick and began writing in the dirt, only for Salari to stop him.

"You know I can't read, right? Father never bothered to teach me."

Jehleen placed a wing over his eyes, shaking his head.

"Kahren, I still don't think it's a good idea," Jallin the Otter stated bluntly.

"Well, somethings going to have to happen sooner or later," came the authoritative reply.

The male syan leaned against the windowsill, staring through the thick glass into the obscuring curtain of rain. Three days had passed since Ela had fallen, and the storm had not abated, to say the least. If anything, it had increased in intensity. What made matters worse was the fact that temperatures outside were falling for winter, causing the already chilling precipitation to freeze on impact. It almost seemed that the storm was a liquid blizzard.

Ela's condition hadn't improved either. Every single older individual in the holt that had any experience with injuries of this magnitude had taken a chance to treat the young adult syan, but nothing had proven effective.

Jallin's mate Jolah, assisted by Roath, did everything in her power to keep the restless little ones occupied toward the back room of the holt, so as not to create unnecessary noise stress on their unconscious elder brother. Artitan would worriedly depart from the group games to join in the vigil in the main hall to see his closest friend and sibling. Occasionally, he would fondly stroke Ela's mane carefully, and would then return to the back with the others. Kahren would watch these affectionate gestures, wishing that he too had a brother.

He soon returned to his concern that his son's time was running out. Despite the promise of the spirit syan Iven, Ela was helpless as ever, showing little power against death. Determined to do something about it, Kahren had made the resolve to return to the Mountain Top with his son, hoping that somehow Iven would return and heal Ela. He had voiced this intention with the others, only to be met with much protest for his and

Ela's safety in the midst of the storm.

For the last few moments a solemn but awkward silence had followed, leaving Kahren to glance again out into the storm. The only noise that broke the still air was made by the squeak of a door hinge as Artitan once more emerged into the main hall to see Ela. Kahren glanced at the reflection of his sons in the window, carefully watching to see that his eldest's condition didn't suddenly become worse. His mate was off in the corner, praying fervently. Heart-wrenching tears freely flowed down her cheeks and muzzle. During this spell of uncertainty, she normally was hunched over her firstborn, but for the time being, she was away to let Artitan take her place at Ela's side.

Noise erupted from the back, drawing attention from the adults as young Jeyla darted into the main chamber. Roath came in after him, trying to halt his run.

"Sorry, Father," she began, but Jeyla cut her off.

"Father, is Ela better?"

The Patriarch glanced to his firstborn, though he already knew the answer. "Jeyla, please..."

"He's not dying, is he?"

The older syan sighed, exchanging glances with his

mate. She nodded as if she read his thoughts.

Kahren motioned to his daughter behind his waiting son. "Bring the others forward. Come, Jeyla."

Artitan stepped aside a moment, allowing his younger brother and Father to stand beside Ela's pale form. Jeyla eyed his eldest brother, his eyes becoming moist. He took his father's paw as his other siblings were ushered in by Roath.

For many moments, the young syans were allowed to speak a few words to their comatose brother. Sela, unable to retain composure near her firstborn, hung back, letting her little ones share what might prove to be their last words to Ela. As each finished, Roath motioned for them to return to the back room, more solemn and obedient than when they came into the main chamber. Jeyla went last, having held his Father' paw the entire time, but reluctantly followed his younger siblings.

Kahren, unable to maintain his gaze on his dying son, returned to the window as Artitan returned to Ela's side. The young lad's hazel eyes stared a long time at the closed eyelids of his stricken sibling.

"Brother," he whispered softly. "Please don't die. Remember what Iven said? We are supposed to help everyone be safe. We need you. *I* need you. You're supposed to be the leader of the Preservants. Please, come back."

Kahren turned, tears trickling down his face. The normally composed syan Patriarch could take it no more.

"Beloved," he said, turning to his mate, "We can't just wait around for something to happen. I have to take him up to the Mountain. Tonight."

She sent a glance with her brow furrowed, her last tear long since shed. "But Kahren, what about the storm?"

"It can last for another week or so," he replied determinedly. "But I'm not letting this storm or even ten others just like it stop me. Our son has a purpose to fulfill, and as he is in his present state, he won't be able to accomplish very much."

"Alright, mate," Jallin the Otter shrugged with uncertainty crossing his features. "How long will it take you to get up to the top?"

The Patriarch syan turned back towards the window.

"Were it just me going at decent speed, alone carrying him, I could do it in a day. But with the elements like this... Only goodness knows."

Chapter 11

Kahren set forth as soon as the environment outside was nearly pitch-black. During the daytime, the clouds high above had glowed faintly in an eerie grayish hue, but darkened as the night came on. Relentless, the storm continued to rage onwards.

The syannic Patriarch would have preferred making this run during the daytime hours, but he had hoped that by nightfall, conditions would have softened. He could not afford for his son's sake to wait until morning. Besides, he knew this trail well. Light or dark, he could still traverse it.

The elder syan held his son's limp form, the body loosely wrapped in a protective cloth to shield Ela from the storm. Kahren dared not to look up towards the peak looming high above him as he walked through the icy saturated turf, the paths little more than freezing mud. Knowing the creek must surely have risen and widened out, he took an alternate course, only guessing just how difficult this journey would be. Lightning flashed high above, lighting the scene with an intense burst, followed almost instantly by the echoing boom of thunder.

The syan, for the first time in many years, was facing this climb alone.

Kahren's mate worriedly watched her beloved and firstborn vanish into the night from the shelter of the window. Her heart wrenched at the prospect of losing them to the storm.

In the midst of her internal fretting, the syanness Matriarch hadn't noticed Jolah the Otter's approach from behind. Slightly startled, she let out a sigh.

"I hope they return safely."

"Oh, don't you worry a thing now, Sela," the female

otter hugged her reassuringly. "From what Jallin tells me, your Kahren can take good care of himself. Now, I don't know what this whole deal with this Iven spirit is, but I'm sure they'll be watched over by the Creator. We just need to be brave, now."

Sela, as she was called, nodded in agreement and sniffled. Turning from the window, she said, "You're right. Come, let's keep the little ones occupied."

Salari sighed glumly as he glanced up the narrow tunnel in the roots of the oak tree. Leading out into the storm that had raged for only goodness knew how long now, he and Jeen had lost all track of time since they had entered into this protective shelter. However, it had been enough time for their collective body heat to warm the entrance chamber of the dwelling, allowing them and their garb to remain dry.

The cavern itself was overall small and cramped, with dozens of side tunnels branching out. The support for the whole structure was the arching roots overhead. Having recovered his sense of smell, Salari detected further evidence that the dwelling had not been inhabited for many seasons. Exactly what kind of creature had lived here was still unknown, as Jeen also could not read, much to Jehleen's exasperation after he tried writing in the dirt with the stick. It was clear they were indeed small and of short stature based on the height of all the storage spaces and other things they found. Jehleen had not been exaggerating at all.

"Any sign of it letting up?"

The Warrior turned to see Jeen come around the corner as she had the last few days now. She had left multiple times to explore the side tunnels, hoping to find something of interest. It seemed her expression that the most recent search was fruitless.

"No," Salari shook his head, his countenance grim. "The storm is insistent as ever. Did you manage to find anything of interest?"

She shook her head. "No, not much. Most of the tunnels just branch off for a distance to empty caverns. However, there are a few that just keep on going. I didn't explore those too far, since the lighting in here is pretty bad."

Salari sighed again, glancing up the entrance tunnel. He turned. "We don't have the time to just wait our tails off down here. We obviously can't go out into the storm, so we might as well try some deep exploring."

Jeen's eyes widened nervously. "Down those longer tunnels? Do you think that's safe? I mean, what if the last inhabitants left because something had collapsed?"

The Warrior made his way towards one of the outbranching tunnels. He beckoned to her confidently. "I'm sure it's safe. I've done exploring before when I was much younger, and my father showed me ways of telling if tunnels are on the verge. I see no danger."

She still looked doubtful, but obediently followed after him. Not wanting to be ignored or left alone, Jehleen stood up and trotted after them.

Neither of the three had noticed the dark beady eyes that had watched them from behind a thin root obscuring a small hidden crevice. Once they were out of sight, a young white-furred creature stepped into the open.

"Wings and invisibility... Strange Ones, aren't they?"

With yet another blinding flash, lightning forked across the sky, leaving the vicious crack of thunder's whip to echo through the clouds. For all eyes beholding the ravaging spectacle, fireworks danced in their vision, leaving all dark surroundings obscured from sight.

Alternating from freezing to hail every few moments, the frigid rain continued its unrelenting torrent, an upheaval of a hurricane-swept ocean that fell from the enshrouded heavens. Many a madbeast would have only stood in the midst of it all, laughing wildly and whooping hysterically at the onslaught; creatures with more sense cowered away in their dens and homes, wishing and waiting for it all to pass.

Through it all, Kahren fought his way bravely up the mountain path amid erratic gusts of wind. Billowing surges blasted the darkened eastern face. The syan, clambering up the sheltered west side, clenched his jaw, straining to keep his own as well as his son's weight moving up the steep incline. Every step came with only the greatest of effort. His strength was already fast waning.

Kahren still did not know what had occurred between Ela's fall and the time he arrived, but that did not matter right then; his son needed help immediately, and nothing would deter him from his course. The syan Patriarch still had a ways to go; he was now only halfway up to the top. And there were still the steep areas to contend with. Had it not been for his strength and experience, Kahren knew he would already be at his knees. He had come too far to just give up now.

Yet again, another barb of lighting shot forth, illuminating Kahren's surroundings. Before the painfully sharp boom of thunder rent the air, he could see several distant trees that had been split or otherwise destroyed by recent strikes from above. With a sudden sinking realization, Kahren knew that once he cleared the trees toward the top, nothing would protect him from being struck by lightning.

A massive bolt whipped in a jagged arc from directly above where the syan stood to a nearby sycamore tree that stood above its companions. Feeling as though his eardrums were about to burst from the explosion of the thunder that immediately followed, Kahren instinctively dropped to the ground in a squat next to a large jutting stone, using his body to shield the comatose form of Ela.

Within a fraction of a second that felt to the syan like an eternity, the sycamore clove open, sending splintery shrapnel in all directions. The tree, being split in two, lost its structural integrity and each half began to topple in its own direction with a painful ear-splitting snapping.

With horror, the syan Patriarch saw the larger portion fall towards him and his son. With little time to react to save them both, Kahren glanced to Ela. Believing his time had come, he touched the lad's mane sorrowfully.

"I'm sorry," was all he could say, just before the charred body of the sycamore tree came crashing down.

The first of the tunnels that Salari, Jeen, and Jehleen choose to explore had started out narrow, but gradually widened out. The Warrior had fashioned a torch out of an old dry root that he had pried out from barring their path a ways back. The hollows had easily ducked under it, but Jehleen was too big to go either over or under. Having also found an old piece of cloth from the previous inhabitants, and equipped with his own flint and tinder, Salari soon had their way brightly lit. Since then, they had trekked on, finding little more than twisted roots and pebbles imbedded along the ongoing walls.

"How far could this tunnel possibly go?" Jeen asked. Salari shook his head with uncertainty.

"I dunno. I'm sure whoever built these tunnels had to stop at some point."

The young Warrior stopped, his senses suddenly alert. Something was different about their surroundings, but he couldn't quite put his paw on it. There wasn't much to see even in the light of the torch, save for dirt. And that was still just the same dark-brown they had seen for the last while.

"What is it?" asked Jeen. "Is something wrong?"

Pausing before answering, he sniffed the air. "Something's changed. I don't know what, though. I don't *think* we're in any danger..."

The Healer shivered slightly. "Did you feel that breeze?"

Before he had the chance to reply, all three were suddenly hit by a blast of icy air that extinguished the torch. Jehleen quickly and instinctively threw each of his wings around the hollows, shielding them from most of the whistling dirge. There was no mistaking the sensation of the chilly white flakes that began to coat their fur and haldrises. Wherever the tunnel was leading them was enshrouded in the midst of winter.

As quickly as it had appeared, the blast of wind died down. Jehleen the Okara lowered his wings, which were covered with a fine icy powder. He shook himself off, spraying the young hollows.

"Hey!" exclaimed Jeen, sending a mock glare at the okara. She then turned to Salari, her expression serious.

"What was that?" she asked.

He glanced at the dead embers of the torch, then down the pathway that lay ahead, colors dancing in his vision. It would be another moment before his dark adaption would set in.

"I don't know," the Warrior replied. "Wait a moment..."

He inspected the walls of the tunnel. To his astonishment, what had been an earthen structure was now ice. A few light taps with a clenched paw revealed that it was completely frozen solid.

Jeen sensed that something was wrong when she saw the expression on Salari's face as he stared down the long corridor. "What is it?"

"I don't quite know," he shook his head with concern. "But from what I can tell..." he paused, unable to bring forth an explanation.

"Salari, what's wrong?" she asked firmly, starting to become afraid.

"Touch the walls," he motioned with a nod.

She obeyed, and let out a horrified gasp, confirming that he wasn't imagining things. She even knocked on it lightly, listening as each rap sounded muted.

"It's ice! Not just a coat, but completely solid! How did this happen so quickly?"

Salari only faced the wall for a moment, sending sidelong glances down both directions of the tunnel. He shook his head, completely bewildered.

"Jeen, Jehleen... I'd hate to say it, but... I think we've stumbled into another tunnel entirely. This one is nothing like where we just were."

The Healer stared at him in complete shock, her mouth agape. "I think you're right... but how is that even possible?"

The Warrior stared down the corridor before them. He motioned them with a wave of his paw, beckoning them to follow after him.

"I think we'd better find out what we're doing here, and quickly. Come, there's only way to go, now."

Chapter 12

Kahren's world was a slow-motion explosion of charred wood splinters and shrapnel, wincing with his eyes tightly shut. He was sure that he and the unconscious Ela were about to meet a grisly fate underneath the falling sycamore in the midst of the horrendous conditions of the storm. The syan felt several of the branches whip across his back, the tree rotating as it fell, like whips leaving lash marks across his hide.

He fought the urge to scream, knowing it would only be in vain. He waited apprehensively for the dreaded sensation of being crushed to be over with. The syan could feel the ground underpaw shuddering noticeably from the impact that was about to inflict death upon him.

But nothing else happened. The crashing noise was quickly drowned out by another burst of thunder, and aside from the stinging scratches received from the twigs, Kahren felt no pain. He opened his eyes and looked up, only to see that the trunk had barely stopped just above, its fall broken by the large stone by which he squatted. He let out a trembling sigh of relief.

The syan inspected his new surroundings. The collapsed sycamore just a hairsbreadth above him provided a little protection from the pouring rain, but not much. He and his son were drenched from head to paw, cold on the stony mountainside, the remainder of their path without protection from lighting, leaving them hopelessly stranded with no chance of relief.

Kahren fell to his knees in despair. It had already taken him a good part of the night to get to this spot. Dawn wouldn't be far off by now, not that it mattered much; he knew that under these conditions, the injured body of his son didn't stand a chance of surviving much longer. The syan Patriarch looked up to the blackened sky above pleadingly as he dropped his upper body weight to his forepaws. Then, drooping his head, he uttered the most fervent petition to the heavens that he could muster. Rainwater ran off his mane as quickly as it fell from above.

"Creator!" he cried over the noise of the storm. "My son was promised power against death. I don't know why this was allowed to happen to him, but if nothing is done soon, he will die! Please, help him! He is my firstborn son. Please, help Ela," he repeated, beginning to sob.

Tears welled up in his eyes. Until that moment, he hadn't realized how much he truly loved his son. It was true he had raised him, taught him wisdom, protected him when he was younger and a little reckless; but never before having come close to this heavy of a loss, he just never considered how much he would miss his firstborn to death, let alone any of his sons or daughters.

Moments of Ela's young life began to flash in Kahren's vision. He recalled with fondness the number of times they had gone fishing together. They had once caught a decently-sized catfish early one morning. At first the young lad had enjoyed the sport, but lost interest when he discovered the fish was dying; but Kahren took the time to tell his son that it would provide their meal.

Ela would still join his father for fishing, but would grow distant and stare out into space while they waited for their fishing lines to be snagged.

This odd behavior of evident pondering would mystify Kahren, but in later seasons he never put much thought into it. In all other respects, Ela was a normal syan. The Patriarch looked over his son's sealed eyes.

"I don't know why everything is happening the way it is, young one. I don't know if you can hear me now, or if you heard some of the things your mother, sister, and brother said; but I want you to know that no matter what happens, I *will* be there. I really hope you make it through all this. But I want you back. You've been a great strength to your mother and me. When your other siblings came along, I always admired how you helped make things easier rather than draw more attention to yourself. I know it hasn't been easy, but I always figured that eventually you would take over leading the family when my time comes."

Kahren's thoughts were also briefly drawn away to his second-eldest son Artitan. He too had an odd quirk, one of being unusually tender-hearted and sensitive to when things were wrong and needed to be fixed, but he typically had his attention more focused than most other creatures that Kahren knew. He smiled sadly as his mind was drawn back to reality.

The first thing that caught his attention was not the storm, but a rather familiar sensation. It began to spread through his body. Filling his entire frame, a warmth gave him strength and overpowered his exhaustion from the strenuous trek up the mountain amid the raging storm. In astonishment and excitement, he looked skyward, just as a light began to bathe him and his son and the ground underpaw. So bright was it against the virtual darkness around him that the syan squinted, covering his eyes.

"It is accepted."

The voice that uttered those words was unlike any Kahren had heard before. It was calm but majestic, and filled him with joy. He knew it was from the Creator. The syan Patriarch's mouth fell open with wonder at this brilliant light, but more so at the fact that he'd heard the Creator Himself speak.

To Kahren, it seemed as though the light that radiated from above and chased away the darkness was filled with calmness, and he thought that he could almost hear an unearthly voice singing from within the folds of the brilliant illumination. What he was now witnessing far surpassed all of his previous visions. Above him, the sycamore trunk seemed to dissolve away.

A sinewy male otter with familiar features led several hundred creatures of numerous kinds of species through an arching portal that stood on grassy flatlands. Many of them Kahren recognized to be from dreams during those horrific fatal battles. These must be the survivors, the syan thought to himself.

Immediately, he beheld the surface of six foreign worlds; the first was of Ice; the second of forest and mountains; the third of wooded wetlands and swamps; the fourth rolling fields of red turf; the fifth of ocean and islands; the sixth and final of rock and sparse shrubbery. Kahren could even see distinctly the inhabitants of those worlds.

And at the center of it all was that familiar face of the otter, only at other times he was also in the form of a squirrel, then a hare, then a hollow, then a gara, amongst other species. At last, Kahren realized who this creature was.

It was Ela!

Though the syan Patriarch thought he saw other

things that he would not recall later, his mind was drawn back to the present reality. He saw in the beam of this light what appeared to be a vine of fire snake and writher its way down towards the syans. In dumb amazement, Kahren watched openmouthed as it angled towards the comatose Ela, alighting itself on his scrawny chest directly over his heart. The vein pulsed and throbbed, seeming as though it were pumping new life into the dying lad.

After a moment that felt as though it were an eternity, the young syan's limp form began to glow with an otherworldly radiance. Ela's frame stiffened, and it looked as though the vein began to lift him into the air from off the ground where he lay. Hovering just a little off the earth, his footpaws hung limp. Strength was returning to the near-lifeless Ela, who suddenly spread his forepaws wide left and right. His head upturned, the young syan's eyes opened. His brow furrowed as he looked around, breathing normally.

At last, Ela was lowered, leaving him to stand upon his footpaws. The pulsing vein of fire retreated from him gradually until it returned from whence it had come. The glow that had radiated from the lad dimmed, leaving him looking as he had before his fall from the cliff. He looked to his father in complete confusion.

He was alive!

Overjoyed, Kahren stood up and embraced his son tightly. Tears of gratitude streaming down his cheeks, the syan Patriarch turned and watched as the beam of light from above began to retract.

"The Little One shall be the source of your greatest joy, as well as your greatest sorrow. Keep him safe."

There was no mistaking where that voice came from. Both syans waited as the last of the unearthly presence of illumination had departed.

Still bewildered, Ela looked to his father. Suddenly, a crack of thunder rang out, and both syans instinctively ducked down. They found themselves back under the protection of the fallen tree leaning on the rock.

Their surroundings had changed back to what it had been before the light had surrounded them. Instead of rain, it was now snowing heavily. All the moisture that had previously poured down was now beginning to freeze upon nearly every exposed surface. The syans' situation looked bleak as Kahren started his son down the path.

"What in the bloomin' name of goodness is going on?" Ela cried out.

What had been mud was now solidifying into hard frozen earth. The wind still lashed about, blasting them aside, every ounce of their effort spent on keeping their course straight. Ela shivered profusely, his teeth chattering. The previously dark environment almost seemed to turn off-white, practically glowing as snow collected on both syans' pelts. They took each other by the shoulder, helping as each stumbled every so often, their paws starting to go numb with cold. No manner of rubbing or blowing on their paws seemed to offer any sufficient relief. Both were trembling, trying to retain enough warmth to make it back home.

"We can discuss it later, son," Kahren replied, taking the blanket he had used for Ela, and draped it over his son once more. "Hurry, we must return down the path to the holt. We won't survive long in this weather!"

Chapter 13

The hollow chieftain Moaren was beginning to be worried. Nearly four days had passed, and there was still no sign of Salari, Jeen, or Jehleen. The young Warrior's father could not deny that they were missing by this point. Surely, they would have already returned if they could have. Something had happened, but no hollow knew what. They were simply gone.

The distant storm witnessed earlier on by the chieftain's mate had spread itself out, and much of the clouds now covered the sky overhead the hollows' domain. Light snow had already begun to fall, heavily signaling the fast approach of winter.

Moaren came to an ultimate decision. He was going to have to find them. Resting on one of the upper boughs of the sarcras tree, he carefully considered the preparation that needed to take place for his journey and tribal absence.

Typical of the nature of his species, his tail was wound several times around his perch for stability. Very little of his appearance distinguished him as a ruler amongst his tribe, save for three small tattooed dots that ran in a crescent arc along the outer edge of his right eye. He wore a garb similar to other hollows, a haldris bearing the symbols that other creatures were incapable of perceiving by sight.

Despite their creepishly vague appearance and hissing speech, hollows were not very deceitful or evil creatures. They were more of a tribal warrior culture that preferred not having too many outsiders constantly watching their every move. Hence, they had made the haldrises to keep attention from being drawn to them; and consequently as a result, the "Strange Ones" became known as the hollows by other creatures.

Chief Moaren continued to glance to the point in the sky where the missing three creatures had last been seen. He knew he would need his best and strongest warriors to go with him on the search. Such a young world was a very dangerous place indeed.

Though Salari kept encouraging his companions on with the prospect of discovering a way out at the end of the tunnel, he knew something was drastically wrong. Ever since the wind had plowed through the corridor earlier, his Warrior instincts were practically screaming at him. Once the blast of air had died down, he knew in a quick glance that a score of paces behind them the tunnel was blocked off. Not by rubble that had collapsed, but they were in a foreign corridor that was clearly not the one they had started down. How it all happened was beyond the young Warrior, and it was starting to make him edgy. Nonetheless, he pushed on, not wanting to reveal their predicament to Jeen. Jehleen on the other paw seemed to already know, but wisely made no move to expose anything either.

"Say, do you feel that?" the pretty Healer asked,

drawing his thoughts back to reality. Sure enough, he did feel it: a chilly breeze of fresh air coming from up ahead. The pace of all three quickened with excitement. The promise of even winter conditions was by far brighter than staying any longer in the gloomy dim confines of the underground.

Soon the hollows and okara were racing one another to be the first to emerge. No one had noticed the small branchoff tunnels that had provided means for the wind to flow through; they didn't care. Freedom was around the corner.

Jehleen attempted to flap his wings to give himself extra momentum, despite the lack of space available. Meanwhile, the young hollows coiled their lengthy tails close to their bodies for warmth. Light began to gradually increase, and their footpaws were beginning to crunch deepening snow on the tunnel floor.

Then they saw it: ahead, a pillar of sunlight shone from a hole in the ceiling, a little narrower than the corridor itself. As their eyes adjusted to what seemed at first to be blinding sunshine, they could see that the hole rested just before the end of the tunnel.

Suddenly widening out into a narrow chamber, the

okara seized the opportunity to get past Salari and Jeen. He leapt over their heads, landing deftly in time to prevent collision with the wall beyond the light. Jehleen then stood upright with his long hind legs springing, thus allowing him to clamber out into the open air. First Jeen, then Salari climbed after him, grabbing to whatever pawholds they could find along the walls. They too emerged, squinting at first as they took stock of their new surroundings.

To their uttermost astonishment, a wide, rolling plain of snow stretched in every direction that they could see. Behind them was a gentle incline of a partially rocky, partially ice-encrusted hill. Besides that, there was little, if any indication of other features; this new realm, wherever they were, was utterly barren. All three suddenly felt very exposed, having spent most of their lives in high-density forests.

"You may think it's not much, but we call it home."

Salari's senses suddenly went alert at the unexpected sound of a nearby voice. Swiveling about, he and his companions saw the source, initially unnoticed.

A score of paces away, several small white foxes stared back at them as though to inspect the hollows. Their fur glinted almost as brightly as the snow in the light of the early afternoon sun. The biggest of them, speaking with an air of authority, spoke inquiringly in a calm but firm voice. Mentally counting them, Salari and Jeen saw eight in all.

"I am Shateel Iceclaw, Chieftain of this realm. We would appreciate if you would be so kind as to reveal your names, as well as why you three have ventured into our domain."

Salari stepped forward between his friends and the white fox and introduced himself. "My apologies if we have trespassed. I am Salari the Warrior. My companions are Jeen the Healer and Jehleen the Okara. We mean no harm by our presence. As to why we are here, a storm drove us to find underground shelter. We explored some tunnels while we waited for the weather to clear, and somehow ended emerging here."

Shateel briefly glanced upon the hole with disdain through narrowed vision. "Indeed. If I may ask, how long were you down there in the tunnel?"

Salari shrugged with a respectful nod. "Alas, I cannot

say for certain, since there was no means of keeping track of time. If I were to wager a guess, I would say perhaps three days."

Shateel's eyes widened slightly in surprise, his ears twitching. "Three days, you say? Have you had any sustenance in that time?"

The Warrior suddenly realized how hungry he was. Due to the storm, there was no shortage of water, but they had also been cut off from food supply. However, since the hollow tribe in the past had gone through periods of little food, Salari and Jeen had found it easier to ignore than most creatures would have. Jehleen, for all he knew, had been nibbling on some of the roots when he wasn't looking.

Salari had only just met these strange creatures standing before him on the opposite side of the hole, but his instincts told him to trust them, despite his initial caution. Respectfully, he shook his head.

"No, we have not," the young Warrior replied.

The fox actually allowed a slight smile of welcome to show on his seemingly sly features. "Then come with us. It is not often we have visitors to dine with."

Salari smiled back. "We appreciate the invitation.

You may wish to watch Jehleen closely, lest he eat you out of house and home. He can pack quite a bit away."

The remark left the hollow to duck as his friend shot in for a sarcastic nip at Salari's pointed eartip.

Many leagues distance from the hollow's woods found a lone solitary gara standing under the pre-dawn stars atop a dry grassy hillside knoll overlooking the bare trees of his forest home. Aka the Seer had made it part of his routine to arise well before the others of his kind to be alone; he preferred it to be such so that he was free to ponder and meditate without interruption as he stood stargazing and star reading.

Much of the time he liked to listen to the stories told by the stars. So many countless other worlds orbited those stars much in the same way the Earth circled her sun in a virtually endless cycle. Nearly all of those worlds were much older that the ground upon which he stood. So many inhabitants; so many stories.

Few creatures ever understood how the Seer thought. His mind was constantly active, his pale blue eyes staring into and through everything. On occasion could he see more than a few years into the future; for the most part, he would listen to the echoes of the past, and watch the present. There were no secret major events that could be hidden from his view. It was as though his head contained the most sophisticated compilation of historic accounts, even for events that had not yet happened.

He saw a world obscured in darkness whose habitants lived in constant peril from storms unlike any other the Seer could fathom. These storms continuously pulsed and throbbed with power, with such brightness that it hurt the pale-eyed gara to watch. Sometimes, though it was always difficult to tell, it almost seemed as though there was another world right next to it, wholly obscured in the glare of the storms that tore across the surface of dust and stone. Massive columns of rock thrust their way upward out of these planes, the only feature marking the otherwise sandy and barren wasteland.

Another world, possessed chiefly by grey-blue cats of incredible longevity, appeared to be a strange kind of lush paradise. Their culture was highly advanced, having developed the ability to construct ships that could actually lift them to other worlds, rather than just float on water. Aka could sense a brewing threat to them that was arising, but what exactly, he could not tell. It was too far into the future to discern.

Despite these and many other old worlds, the Seer's attention was drawn to a distant trouble on his own. Sensing that something big was fast approaching, his curiosity was piqued. He began to try to search out what.

Death.

Dread.

War.

Nothing distinct came. His vision of what was to come was naught but vague despite his prying efforts. Aka narrowed his eyes in irritation, and turned up to the stars.

The dark sky stared back at him apathetically. In the eastern horizon, Aka the Seer noticed for the first time the ominous line of storm clouds gathered together, the gara did not need his gift to know that it was going to be severe when it finally struck. Rather than immediately turning to leave, he stood to watch as it spread its way through the sky.

Aka stared at the ground a moment. To him, the cruelest irony was knowing everyone around him so well, but few knew the slightest thing about him beyond his gift. The only one who came remotely close was his mate Jalo-in. She somehow managed to pry. Well before she knew that star reading existed, well before they became mates, she had caught his eye as one who just knew what questions to ask.

Thinking of his mate suddenly reminded Aka that until she learned some of his gifts for her own use, she was oblivious to the oncoming storm. The gara quickly rose, snatching his staff. He hurried to the grove of trees, knowing the storm was fast approaching.

Making his way to the proper tree, he clambered up, his staff between his teeth. Reaching the first limb, he hunkered down, taking the staff in his left paw. The gara slowly hopped forward toward the bundle before him. He nudged her.

"Jalo-in. Shh, slowly. Do you want to see a storm?"

The female squinted her eyes at him. "Why would I want to see anything at this hour?"

"Sorry, I should have worded that differently. Do you wish to see a great storm under *protection*?"

Detecting the hint, she suddenly got quiet and rose

up. Taking her paw in his, Aka led his mate to another nearby limb, where two forms were curled up. The male gara took a piece of bark lying near his paws, and tossed it toward the pair.

"Malyth. Yase. Come."

The younger male, springing awake, bit his tongue when he heard his brother's voice. He ushered to his new mate Yase, the pair only having made their commitments the night before. Both mystified clambered after the Seer.

Aka led them to the top of the tree, motioning with his staff toward the rolling masses that bellowed toward the grove. "The others. The Preservants. They're in there."

Malyth squinted. "You woke us up at this hour to tell us that? You've got to kidding...!"

Aka motioned with his staff. "Keep it down. I woke you so that the storm wouldn't. Come, there's a space in one of the trees that we can occupy until it passes."

Yase paused. "But what of the others? Shouldn't we warn them?"

The Seer looked aside, setting his staff upright. "We could. Or we could get a head start on learning our gifts as Preservants.”

Malyth sneered. “Sure we could. And I suppose you’ll help us figure that out?”

“I’ll do better. I will show you!”

Moments later found them cramming into the narrow crevice of a hollowed-out tree that most of the older gara had forgotten about. The space within wasn’t terribly cramped, but they were close together. The Seer raised his staff and rolled his wrist, creating a small circle with the top. He tapped the bottom on the wood floor, watching as the other three sets of eyes followed the motions in the dark.

“I will show you all what your respective tasks will be. Malyth, you are the Rogue.”

“Sure, of course I am.”

“Let me finish! Your task encompasses that of leveler. You will challenge everything.”

Jalo-in rolled her eyes. “As if he doesn’t already.”

Yase smacked her paw. “*Your* mate isn’t finished speaking!”

The Seer continued before any further argument could erupt. “As a leveler and challenger, you will ensure that everything of importance is maintained, for they alone will withstand your challenging. All else will fail. Yase, you are Vixen. You will aid Rogue in his charge, and will also rein him in when he goes too far. You will help those who may be affected by his actions. Jalo-in, you are Accountess. Your task is to keep all of us in check. Though you are not leader, you will serve as the chief of reason."

Jalo-in shook her head, her expression puzzled. "Why would that not fall to you?"

The Seer dipped his head. "Seeing everything is one thing. Having the wisdom to make the correct decision in all cases? You're far better gifted for that than I am. And of course, my task speaks for itself."

Malyth scoffed. "You said you'd show us our tasks. All you've done is tell us about them."

Seer lowered the top of his staff, gently touching each of the others on the head. "I have told you. Now you will see it."

Malyth grunted, and then his expression changed as he fell into a trance. His mate followed suit, Jalo-in starting gaze into space.

"What's happening?"

"As I said... I am showing you. What you're about to

Michael Andrew McDonald

see is part of the future."

With that, the Seer closed his eyes.

Chapter 14

Back at the syan's holt, the older and younger generations alike stood dumbstruck as they witnessed through the single windowpane the spontaneous blizzard that had erupted outside. The storm had transitioned from pelting rain to fat snowflakes suddenly and without warning of any kind. It didn't take long for all present to worried glances about the fact that Ela and Kahren were still out there, doubtlessly caught in the thick of the freak storm.

Jallin was the first to speak. He stared sternly out the window.

"Ho, no, you don't," he muttered. "If those two don't

return soon, I'm going out after them."

Sela's eyes widened. "Jallin, we don't need another creature to be compromised out there!" she protested. "Kahren will find his way back soon enough, he's done it scores of times! I just hope he is successful with getting Ela recovered. I hope they're both alright."

"Aye, that's true," the burly male otter nodded. "But not under these conditions. The snow's comin' down so thick, I think they soon won't be able to see their own paw if it were placed in front of their face. Besides, I can't just stay around here like some useless lump running your larder storage of food down. I've got to be doing something."

His mate patted his shoulder reassuringly. "You've been helping out around the holt. That's better than stranding yourself to a cold death."

He bobbed his head uncertainly. "It's only if they're not back quickly. Remember, our fur is denser, and I'm strong enough to carry them both back if need be. I stand a better chance of surviving that mess than Kahren, and especially Ela. Oh, sorry, Sela, I didn't mean..."

The syanness shook her head, turning her head away momentary as she ran a paw under her eye. "It's alright.

Kahren will find his way back. The Creator didn't give me a weak or cowering mate."

Jallin's mate glared at him, the male otter helpless to do anything but shrug. "I'm sorry, it's just that I hate feeling useless when there's something to be done. Even if... I mean *when*, Kahren can make it himself."

Not paying much attention to the conversation, Roath glanced out the window. At first it seemed the storm was playing tricks on her as the flurries rushed past, but she looked more closely and sure enough saw that there was a movement outside contrary to the commotion of the storm. Suddenly, two snow-plastered figures materialized out of the fog, fighting their way to the holt. Roath jumped excitedly back from the window and began to cry out.

"Father and Ela are back! They're alright! Hurry, open the door for them!"

The door swung in as Jallin yanked it hard with a tingle of anxiety that was causing his paws to shake. The otter was greeted with an explosion of snowflakes blasting their way in, quickly accompanied by two syans that appeared in the opening. The entrance was as quickly shut as it was opened. Kahren and Ela stood with their paws folded tightly, teeth chattering together as they shivered profusely.

"Ela! You're alive!" Roath cried out, her voice a mix of confusion and joy. Their mother appeared on the scene, a hefty blanket in each paw, discarding the ice-encrusted one over Ela's shoulders. Both of the syans were promptly bundled and ushered over to the crackling fireplace, the last few logs of wood greedily being consumed by the licking of flames.

As they warmed themselves, brushing off snow, Jallin remarked, "It doesn't look like you had too much fun makin' snow angels out there, did you, Kahren?"

The syan Patriarch irritably glowered back. "I'd like to see you try it sometime! Your thick heavy pelt will probably allow you to stay out for hours. Perhaps we should go ahead and give it a go?"

"Enough of this," Sela intervened. "Jallin, I don't think Kahren is in the mood for jesting. He gets like this after... certain things happen." Turning to her mate, she asked, "Beloved, will you tell us how Ela was brought back?"

Still shivering, Kahren turned his attention from the warmth of the fire. "All I can say is that we never made it to the top. It's not an account for me to tell." He glanced to his eldest son. "It is his."

Ela suddenly felt very self-conscious when he sensed the half-dozen sets of eyes behind him focusing in on him. The lad had allowed his mind to wander as he gazed into the flames of the fire, holding loosely to the blanket draped over his shoulders, up until his subconsciousness heard his father referring to him. He turned his head to see them all watching expectantly. Hesitant at first, he cleared his throat, ordering his thoughts.

"I don't know what all happened, but the last thing I remember was running home from the stormclouds with father and Alam. The next thing I knew, everything went black for a moment. I became aware of an awful pain all over me. I thought I saw a spirit of some kind standing over me that tried to help, but for some reason, appeared afraid. He vanished right before I passed out again.

"After that, all I can recall is hearing a beautiful sound, sort of like a distant singing choir, and then I found myself standing in the air over father, the pain disappearing right there. Whatever was holding me up lowered me until I was next to father. Both of us were surrounded by some sort of brilliant light that quickly vanished. It all happened so fast, I can barely remember much. It's all so hard to describe, anyhow."

Kahren couldn't hear much of what his son said after he heard the part about a spirit standing over his son immediately following his fall. His mind was instantly drawn back to the scene at the side of the creek. He *knew* he recognized those distinctive pawprints nearby. The syan was getting a sinking feeling in his stomach as the pieces began to fit together.

Meanwhile, a deep silence fell over the holt after listening about the incident. No one had ever heard of anything like what Ela had described, since Kahren had not told much of his experiences over the seasons. Even Artitan, despite his encounter, was speechless, for having his brother so close to death and then brought back so quickly was nothing short of a marvelous miracle.

Kahren finally broke the silence by leaning over and whispering something inaudible to the others into Ela's ear. The lad turned to his father and gave a quick nod. Unexpectedly, the Patriarch froze, his face beginning to pale. The onlooking spectators could tell that something was clearly amiss.

Sela stepped forward. "Is something the matter, Beloved?"

Kahren turned to his kin and the otters in shock. "Indeed, something is very wrong." He glanced out toward the storm. "There's someone trapped out in the storm that shouldn't be here in this area."

"Who?" asked Jallin.

The reply sent a chill down the spine of Sela and the otters:

"Moaren's son."

Roath and Ela seemed puzzled.

"What's wrong with Moaren's son?" the young male asked. "Who is Moaren, anyway?"

Kahren's gaze met the flames in the mantle. "He is a very honorable warrior of the hollows, and my friend. His son I imagine is likewise. But last we saw one another, Moaren did not ever want to see me alive again."

"What happened?" asked Roath.

"It's a long story," Sela replied. "One that I hope we never have to tell."

Kahren shook his head. "If it was a singular sighting,

then all will be right; but if this is just the first of several, then I fear that the storm outside will pale against when Moaren is through with us."

Outside, the icy dirge continued to rage on ruthlessly. A long, cold, harsh winter was just beginning.

Contrary to what Kahren thought, Salari was nowhere near the syan's holt. True to Kahren's suspicions, the hollow Warrior and his companions were on another world entirely, having unwittingly stumbled through a rift that connected their home to a realm enshrouded in ice quite permanently.

The white foxes led the hollows and okara over several frozen ridges of stone that jutted out of the snowy planes like suspended motionless waves of the ocean. It was atop these ridges they walked, where there was little depth of snow for them to pad through. Salari, Jeen, and Jehleen had quite a wide view of their surroundings given them for quite a distance.

The sun shone dimly toward the horizon in the pale blue sky. Thin wispy clouds hung low in the west where the sun would be in just a few short hours. In the distance, a chain of steep mountains lined the south, the east virtually featureless and the north covered in gentle rolling hills that stretched for leagues beyond. Above them, to their astonishment, a large pale, almost moonlike crescent hovered, a thin partial ring of similar hue arched around, pointing at an angle slightly off angle from the sun. From everything they had seen thus far, this world was quite different from their own. Salari knew Jeen should have surely suspected something by now regarding their vast change in location. His stomach twisted in a knot when she began speaking to the leader of the foxes as they walked, knowing that she was going to ask before too long.

"Shateel Iceclaw—" she began.

"Don't waste your breath, Strange One," he politely interrupted, sending her a glance of acknowledgement. "Shateel will do. Iceclaw is only for enemies and those we don't yet consider friends. Now, continue."

The Healer gave a respectful nod. "Very well, Shateel. If you don't mind my asking, where exactly are we?"

He stopped suddenly, and sent another glance to the hollows and okara before turning his narrowed eyes upward. "It's hard to say, exactly. Where were you before?”

“Do you mean the tunnels?” Jeen asked, having stopped in her tracks as well. The other seven foxes continued on, leaving their leader with their guests.

“No...” He took a deep breath, still gazing toward the sky above, his vision fixated upon the crescent of the orb. “I mean, where did you come from, your home? Describe it to me.”

Salari was the one to answer: “We came from a forest near a wetland. Our home is in the midst of numerous trees, more than can ever be counted. We stay primarily in the branches and boughs, coming to the ground only when we need to.”

“Trees...” Shateel sighed. “It has been so long since I have seen any. I hope you both won’t miss them too much. You’re about to get used to staying away from home for a long time.”

“Why do you say that?” asked Jeen. Already knowing the answer Salari’s hearts began to beat faster nervously.

“My family and I happened upon a small cave one winter a long time ago. The heavy storms that suddenly appeared left us to find no other form of shelter. Venturing deeper in to get away from that blizzard, we emerged from the end of a tunnel, and found ourselves here. Expecting the storm to be over after a time, we tried to return, only to find our path blocked by a wall. We were trapped. It was from that very tunnel you emerged. It took us too long to admit to ourselves that we had somehow been sealed in a new realm, and that returning home was impossible. Every so often we try, to no avail."

Jeen looked to the distant dark range as though the mountains had an answer. "How? And more importantly, why?"

Shateel's eyes narrowed. "Whatever the reason, we are on another world. Whatever dangers you were used to back home have no meaning here. And what dangers you could not imagine now will become your constant companion. That is, depending on if our luck wanes."

Salari looked on ahead, and could see a distant hole that the foxes' tracks led away from. "Is that your dwelling?"

The white fox nodded. "That is where we presently make our home."

Jeen gazed back the way they had come, and then looked over the foxes. "That's quite a distance you covered to merely meet us."

Shateel sighed. "It wasn't you we were seeking. Have you seen a young fox like us?"

The hollows shook their heads.

The fox glanced back over their fresh tracks. "Then we will have to search for my son another day. It is getting too late now to continue to search without a definite sign of his whereabouts."

Epilogue

Nighttime of the next evening had fallen over the syannic holt. Complete exhaustion having fallen upon everyone, all were sound asleep. All except one. Outside, the blizzard continued to rage on.

In the midst of fitful dreams, Ela tossed and turned in his cot. Strange scenes flashed in his mind, everything blurred and alluding. Trapped in the world of his own subconscious, the young syan fought to make sense of what was happening.

Ela found himself in the middle of a wide grassy field, forming a shallow dip in which he stood. Above, it was dark, the stars glittering brightly like jewels studded on the inside of a black velvet cloak. A massive glowing arch that appeared almost like suspended water stood a league from him in the distance. However, to his astonishment, he beheld that within the arch, it was broad daylight.

He thought he heard a sudden whisper calling out to him, and turned. As he looked around to spot the source of the voice, his environment had changed. His puzzled hazel eyes darted, seeing that he was now at the base of a massive sand dune at midday, though the glaring sun beat no heat down on his brow. The towering mound had a set of pawprints studding a path up to the top.

"Ela."

Hearing the whispered voice speak again, it sounded as though it came from the other side of the dune. An inner instinct driving him to seek out and meet who was calling him pushed the young syan to begin making his way up after the strange set of tracks.

With every step forward, he slid back several inches. Each stride seemed to make little, if any, progress. Exhaustion and fatigue setting in, his frustration began to rise. Nonetheless, Ela pushed on. The urge to find the source of what was calling him grew increasingly stronger the closer he got.

At long last, he finally reached the top. To his horror, rather than seeing anyone there, the whole view before him was many more sand dunes just like the one upon which he had just clambered. Beyond, at the very edge of the horizon, were the distant peaks of mountains. Almost immediately, Ela found himself standing atop the highest of them. Before him lay a vast world stretching to a misted horizon; the incline down before him induced wooziness despite that his species were made for mountains. He felt one slip from his perch and he would go tumbling down the steep rock face for several days before he reached the base.

How he got there, he knew not. All he wanted in that moment was to know why he was there.

"Ela."

The voice sounded again, this time louder. Hearing it come from behind, the syan lad turned around quickly. There before him stood a very familiar spirit.

"Iven!" Ela nodded respectfully. "What is going on here? Where am I?"

The spirit turned his head and gazed over the

surrounding landscape opposite the direction the young syan had been looking. With a wave of his illuminated paw, he motioned Ela to join him. The lad obeyed, stepping up to his side.

Before them lay an unobstructed view of a valley forest below, the field of dunes to their backs. Twin Mountains, one just a little larger than the other, rested on the far side of the valley. A winding river snaked its way through the trees and ran down the middle of the area twixt the peaks. Beyond it all lay a distant shoreline waveswept by an astounding blue ocean that stretched to the edge of the horizon.

Ela stood looking in awe for a moment. "Where are we?" he asked, exhaling softly.

Iven continued to gaze over the wooded country below. "This is the site of many great and future events. Ela, you are currently on another world separate of your own."

Ela's eyes widened. "This is another world? But it looks so familiar!"

"For several reasons," Iven nodded affirmatively. "This world once was part of your own. For a time, this one and others have been separated from one another

into seven parts. Your Mother and Father have told you of the Beginning, in which there was a great quaking of the ground. That was the moment in which the world was divided into those quarters. You reside on the largest. The other reason for familiarity is that you have seen this place before you were born."

"Before I was born?" Ela repeated. The young syan's brow furrowed in confusion.

"Aye," Iven replied. "In a way, I am as you were when you were shown this place; an immortal soul waiting to be given a body."

"But why do I not remember any of it, then?" asked Ela. "You're implying that my soul existed for a long time before now, are you not?"

"That is correct." Iven stared forward for a couple heartbeats, and then turned to face the puzzled look on his embodied companion's countenance. He continued.

"Back when you were but a spirit, Ela, you were shown many of the difficulties that you would endure. The Creator wiped your memories of nearly everything, to prevent you from avoiding needed experiences. Otherwise, you would never learn from them. Now, you may fear that your time will be hard, but it is largely to *the contrary. You will be very, very protected from many things. What hard times you do suffer will ultimately work for your good. Worry not. The Creator has great things in store for you."*

"What things?" Ela's ears perked in attention.

Iven flashed a slight smile. "Only Time Will Tell."

Then Ela awoke. *Where am I?* he thought at first, blinking sleep from his eyes as he sat up. He glanced out the single window of the room where he and his siblings slept, and saw that the horrendous storm outside had finally abated. Snow was piled up deeply, covering a depth up to the chest of a male otter. Ela ran a paw through his mane as realization that he had just had a dream dawned upon him. The syan removed his covers as he swung his footpaws gently to the floor, quietly enough not to disturb his brothers and sisters. He stood up and padded noiselessly over to the window.

Exhaling softly, his breath misted on the glass as he leaned in close. The stormclouds had already begun to retreat west, leaving a clear dark patch of night sky in its wake. The stars twinkled and danced wildly with the cool currents of air that bent and distorted the path of the thin streams of light as the wind blew in the upper atmosphere. Ela watched it all passively, deep in thought. So many things had happened lately, that the young syan could hardly believe that nearly a week had passed since his life had begun to change so dramatically. He doubted that his life would ever again be the same.

Little did he have any idea how right he was.

To Be Continued...

Michael Andrew McDonald

-196-

-197-

Michael Andrew McDonald

-198-

Visit the Currenteers' Facebook at

https://www.facebook.com/TheStarCurrent/